TRUE LOVE WAYS

When Meredith Bradbourne returns to Midchester to care for her Aunty Peg, she meets attractive and trendy vicar Drew Cunningham, who uses rock 'n' roll to spread the word of God. Meredith also becomes embroiled in a mystery involving a former policeman. As Meredith and Drew compete as village sleuths, they must also fight their growing feelings. Set against the backdrop of 1950s Britain, *True Love Ways* invokes a more innocent era where darkness lurked behind every net curtain.

SALLY QUILFORD

TRUE LOVE WAYS

Complete and Unabridged

LINFORD
Leicester

First published in Great Britain in 2013

First Linford Edition
published 2014

A catalogue record for this book is available
from the British Library.

ISBN 978–1–4448–2119–2

Published by
F. A. Thorpe (Publishing)
Anstey, Leicestershire

Set by Words & Graphics Ltd.
Anstey, Leicestershire
Printed and bound in Great Britain by
T. J. International Ltd., Padstow, Cornwall

This book is printed on acid-free paper

1

'I'm sorry to do this, Peg, but it's not safe for Meredith to live with you.' Sheila bundled a sleepy twelve-year-old Meredith into her thick duffle coat. 'You're coming to live with me and Uncle Norman for a while, darling. You'll have lots of other children to play with in Sheffield.'

'She's got children to play with here,' said Peg. 'Don't take her, Sheila.' There was something pathetic in Peg's voice. It was many years before Meredith recognised it as the fear of loneliness.

Sheila turned to her sister, and her expression softened. 'I know it's not your fault, love. You just can't help yourself when it comes to murder. But it's not safe for Meredith. You must see that.'

'Are you saying you don't trust me around her?'

'As I said, it's not your fault.'

Peg put a hand on Meredith's shoulder, gently brushing back a wisp of strawberry blonde hair that covered the child's green eyes. 'You be good for your Aunty Sheila and Uncle Norman. Promise you won't forget your old Aunty Peg.'

Meredith threw her arms around her aunt. 'I won't. I've had the best time ever with you, hunting murderers.' Sheila pursed her lips, and made a small 'pft' sound. 'You will let me know who murdered Colonel Trefusis, won't you, Aunty Peg?'

'I don't think that will be necessary,' said Sheila. 'I'll write to you and let you know how she's doing, Peg.' Sheila kissed her sister. 'I do love you, you know that, dear. But we promised Mary we'd take care of her.'

'I've never done anything less, Sheila, but it isn't always possible to shield children from horror. Surely the Blitz taught us that.' The two women were silent for a moment. As young as she was, Meredith knew they were remembering the beautiful sister they'd lost during the early years of the war. They turned with tearstained eyes to the child who was made in her image.

'She'll have a stable home with me and Norman.'

'I know.'

After one last hug from Aunty Peg, Meredith followed Sheila down the garden path and into Uncle Norman's waiting car. She pressed her face against the window, trying to get a last glimpse of Aunty Peg and the cottage. Both were lost in the darkness.

1959

It wouldn't be too bad if there were not so many changes, thought Meredith, as she hauled her suitcase over the footbridge at Stockport Station. It would be even better if the porters weren't all busy helping other passengers. She had about five minutes to get to platform four and catch the Midchester train, otherwise she'd have to wait another hour. If only Aunty Sheila hadn't insisted on her packing so much.

'Aunty Sheila, it's June. I can't see I'll need that many sweaters.' Meredith had removed five sweaters, leaving only her favourite green one.

'You never know, dear,' Aunty Sheila had said, putting the sweaters back in the suitcase. 'I've known it snow in June.'

It was one of those things people always said, but which, as far as Meredith knew, was not true. Perhaps, she thought idly as she lugged her suitcase up the next set of steps, it had snowed in June once, about a thousand years ago, and the story had just continued through the generations, so that everyone believed they'd seen snow in summertime. As she daydreamed, her suitcase caught on a step, and the force flung the lid open, discarding

4

sweaters and more personal items down the steps. 'Oh, damn!'

A man who had been walking behind Meredith stopped, and started picking up items. 'Here,' he said. 'Let me help you.' He was about thirty-five, tall, with fair hair and blue eyes. Very handsome in a clean-cut way that was rare amongst all the teddy boys and James Dean clones that filled the streets of Britain in the late nineteen fifties.

'Thanks, really there's no need to . . . ' She became flustered when he picked up one of her bras. Not least because she suddenly noticed he was wearing a dog collar. 'Sorry about the bad language, vicar,' she said. She mentally filed him as unavailable, which she had to admit made him seem even more attractive than ever.

'Don't worry. You should hear me when I catch my finger in the door.' He handed Meredith her things, and she bundled them into the suitcase, and pressed the lid shut. He held it down for her whilst she fastened the lock.

'Are you expecting bad weather?' he asked. 'With all those sweaters I mean.'

'No, but my Aunty Sheila is.' Meredith grimaced.

'Oh yes, well, Aunty Sheilas tend to know about these things.'

'Don't tell me you've got one.'

'I have, but she's called Gloria.'

Meredith smiled. 'She probably loves you very much though, hence all the fussing. Oh, I'm going to miss the train.'

'Which one are you catching?'

'Midchester.'

'Me too,' he said, picking up her suitcase. 'So let me help you. I'll go ahead and make sure it doesn't leave.' Without waiting for an answer, he walked ahead with long strides. From behind he looked like a panther on the prowl, and it occurred to Meredith that there must be something in the Bible about vicars not being so attractive.

If she secretly hoped he would sit near to her on the train, she was to be disappointed. He kindly helped her to

6

her carriage, putting her suitcase up onto the rack, then smiled his goodbye and disappeared into the crowds at the lower end of the train. She settled back, and thought about poor Aunty Peg.

They had been sitting around Uncle Norman's hospital bed when the news came. Aunty Sheila had rushed home from work, picked up some letters, then dashed straight to the hospital. 'Aunty Peg has broken her ankle,' she said, reading from the letter. 'She says not to worry. She's got a nurse in. But I should go to her. If only Uncle Norman . . . ' She looked at her husband with the mixture of sympathy and irritation that only Sheila could manage. 'You would pick this week to have your gall bladder out,' she said.

'Sorry, Sheila,' he said.

'I'll go and stay with her,' said Meredith. 'I don't start my job at the new school till September.'

'No, that's not necessary, Meredith.' Sheila pursed her lips in the manner that was almost a trademark to her.

7

'Aunty Sheila, I'm a grown-up now. I can take care of myself. And Aunty Peg won't be doing much sleuthing with a broken ankle.'

Sheila sniffed. 'I wouldn't put it past her.'

'Let her go, Sheila,' said Norman. Uncle Norman did not stand up to his wife very often. He liked a quiet life. Strangely enough, when he did, Sheila seldom argued.

'Very well, but don't go getting involved in any mysteries. How Aunty Peg hasn't got herself murdered by now, I don't know.'

So here she was, thought Meredith, a wave of excitement passing over her. On her way to see Aunty Peg for the first time in fourteen years. She had missed her more than she ever admitted to Sheila. Aunty Peg wrote, but unfortunately when Meredith was a child, Sheila got hold of the letters first, so by the time Meredith read them, all the juicy bits were struck out with thick black ink. She had held them up to the light, but to no avail. After a while, Aunty Peg must have realised her letters were being censored, so they had become shorter, and full of less exciting news, until the past few years when they had all but ceased. Meredith felt sad to think that the bond she had once had with her aunt was broken. She hoped that the next couple of months would go some way to rebuilding it.

The carriage began to fill up. There was a middle-aged man in his fifties, with a quiet, scholarly air about him. She had the feeling she had seen him before, but could not remember where. It did not surprise her that he wore a dog collar. He was with a woman in her mid-forties. A real looker, as Uncle Norman would say. She had blonde hair, and was dressed elegantly in a blue silk dress, wearing a white scarf, covered in strawberries around her neck. They seemed to be with another woman, who was rather less elegant. She wore a thick grey coat of which Aunty Sheila would have approved, but which was unsuitable for the humid weather. Her short, dark brown hair, under a mustard-coloured scarf, was clean, but lank. The woman in the strawberry scarf could have taught her a lot about sex appeal.

'Of course,' the drab woman was saying as they entered the carriage, 'you'll have your own way of doing things, Mrs. Mortimer.'

'I'm quite happy to leave the housekeeping to you, Edith. At least until we move on to Peter's new parish. I'm not much of a housewife, as I warned Peter before we married. That was when he told me what a wonder you are.' She looked with fondness at the middle-aged vicar. The woman called Edith did too. 'And do call me Clarice.' Clarice smiled in a way that took in everyone in the vicinity, even those not in her small group.

They were followed into the carriage by two boys and a girl. The boys were teddy boys, each wearing a dark suit with a long coat, drainpipe trousers, and suede shoes with thick crêpe soles. Their hair was slicked back, with a quiff at the front. From what Meredith could make out, one was called Jimmy and the other Bert. The girl was called Betty. Like Clarice she was blonde, but the girl's hair owed more to a bottle. It was styled in the way made famous by Marilyn Monroe, and it seemed clear that Miss Monroe was Betty's heroine. She wore a tight striped top, with a black pencil skirt and dangerously high heels. The look was slightly spoiled by a ladder in the top of her stocking.

'I hope you've brought something proper to wear for strawberry picking, Betty,' said Jimmy.

'I've got my jeans,' said Betty, touching up her blood-red lipstick.

'Good, because we don't want a repeat of last time, when your stilettos got caught in the mud.'

'We should have left her there,' said Bert.

'Hey, you don't talk about my girl like that,' said Jimmy. He pulled a flick

11

knife out of his pocket. Everyone in the carriage held their breath, whilst he sat there opening and closing it for the next five minutes. His eyes gleamed as he looked around, clearly content with the effect he was having on them all.

The final arrival in the carriage was an elderly man. He took the window seat opposite Meredith.

'Sorry, Miss,' he said, stretching out his legs so that Meredith had to pull hers in. 'Got shot in the war. Can't bend this knee at all.' His voice boomed out in the carriage. Meredith pegged him as being ex-military.

'Was that the Boer War, granddad?' asked Bert, sniggering.

'No, it was the Great War,' said the old man. 'Some of us have had to fight for others' freedom to wear stupid clothes.'

'Hey . . . ' Jimmy sat forward. He still held the flick knife, though the blade was tucked away.

'That's enough, Jimmy.' The voice came from the doorway. Meredith looked up to see the young vicar who had helped her with her suitcase.

'Oh, hello, Drew,' said Jimmy, quickly putting the knife into his pocket. 'What you doing on this train?'

'On my way to Midchester, like you.'

'You're not checking up on me, are you?'

'Not everything in life is about you, Jimmy.' The man called Drew smiled. Meredith wondered how difficult it would be to become a born-again Christian. 'I'm going there on church business.'

At that, the older vicar, Mr. Mortimer, stiffened. 'Are you the Reverend Andrew Cunningham by any chance?' he asked.

'Yes, that's right.'

'Peter Mortimer.' Mortimer held out his hand. 'Vicar of this parish. Well, Midchester parish, at least.'

'Ah, it's you I'm coming to see. Nice to meet you, Peter.' The two men shook hands.

'We don't hold with vicars using their

first names in Midchester,' said Edith, sniffing loudly. 'It doesn't instill respect. I daresay you're one of those progressive types, letting this young man call you Drew.'

'Guilty as charged,' said Drew. 'The church is becoming irrelevant in this day and age. It's up to us to make it relevant again.'

Clarice looked at Drew with obvious appreciation, as did Meredith and young Betty.

'Drew is brilliant,' said Betty. 'He's kept Jimmy out of trouble.' She looked proud, though what there was about the menacing Jimmy to be proud of, Meredith was at a loss to understand.

'I'd like a chat with you, Drew,' said Peter Mortimer. 'Perhaps we could go along to the buffet car. You don't mind, do you, darling?'

'Not at all,' said Clarice. 'Edith and I can have more time to get to know each other.' Meredith noticed an underlying tone in Clarice's voice, suggesting that it was not high on her list of priorities.

Not that she blamed her. Edith clearly had no sense of humour. She reminded Meredith of an early Christian martyr. It would no doubt be the happiest day of Edith's life if she were burned at the stake for her beliefs. As the two men left, Clarice said to Edith, 'It was so good of you to come and meet us at Stockport.'

'I had shopping to do, so I thought I'd wait till you and Reverend Mortimer got back. Was the cruise nice?'

'Oh yes, it was wonderful.'

'Lots of dancing and drinking, I shouldn't doubt.' Edith looked horrified and hopeful at the same time.

Clarice laughed. It was a deep, throaty laugh, and caught the attention of both Jimmy and Bert. Despite the fact she was at least twenty years older than the boys, they were not averse to her charms. 'Yes, Edith,' said Clarice, winking. 'Lots of dancing and drinking. Not to mention all the fornication.'

Edith harrumphed and Meredith looked resolutely out of the window until she trusted herself not to laugh.

After a short time, Reverend Mortimer and Drew returned. The Reverend took his seat, whilst Drew stood resting against the door. There were no other seats for him to take in the carriage. They discussed common-place parish issues, like sermons and the best way to help parishioners.

'Are you travelling far?' It took a moment for Meredith to realise that the old soldier opposite was speaking to her.

'I'm getting off at Midchester. What about you?'

'Hereford. I'm going home. I've just been to a family funeral in Newcastle. Haven't seen my brothers since nine-teen fourteen, just before we all went off to war.'

'It must have been nice seeing them all again.'

'Oh yes. I married a Hereford girl, you see, and we made our home there. I was in the police force until ten years ago.'

16

'Really. You must have had some interesting cases. Murders and things.'

'Not that I can talk about,' said the old man, clamping his lips together.

'No, of course not.' Meredith felt chastened.

'I mean, I can't give proper details, such as when, where or who.'

'Of course, I understand.'

'Unless it's a famous case. Out there in the public eye, as it were. There's a lot go unsolved. Of course we always know who did it, but it's getting the evidence. Like I knew all along that this man had murdered his wife, but he had a solid alibi. Straight and upright sort of man, too. That's why he got away with it. No doubt he's married again now, and maybe she'll meet a sticky end. Another one we fancied the housemaid for it, but there was no motive. We think the old girl said she was going to leave the maid something in her will, and the girl thought she'd done it, then got a bit impatient. Children are the worst though.'

'What? Murderers?' It seemed unlikely to Meredith.

'Oh yes. Evil little blighters, some of them. We never had children, my wife and I. That's because I saw too much. I said to her, 'Myrtle, if we have kids, they'll stab us in our beds'.'

Meredith had a moment's sympathy for poor childless Myrtle. 'But what makes you think that?' she asked the old man. 'Children are so innocent.'

'Don't you believe it.' He tapped the side of his nose. 'Knew a case once — no names, no pack drill mind you. One parent confessed and hanged for killing the other parent. But I knew it was the child. Evil little so-and-so. Had a way of looking at you.'

'What became of the child?' asked Meredith.

'Lord knows. Sent off to live with some relatives, looking innocent as a babe in arms.'

'Well let's hope they never killed again.'

'Don't you believe it, miss. Someone

kills once, they go and do it again. Like one case, a teenager stabbed a dozen people before we caught him. Then he went and escaped. For all we know he could be killing still.'

'We should get Peg Bradbourne on the case,' said Peter Mortimer. It was only then that Meredith realised the whole carriage had stopped to listen to the old policeman. Drew looked at Meredith and raised his eyes heavenward. She sensed he didn't believe a word the old man said.

'You know Peg Bradbourne?' asked Meredith.

'Why yes, she lives in Midchester. Why, do you?'

'She's my aunty.'

'Goodness, you're not little Meredith, are you? Mary's girl?'

'Yes, that's right.'

'Do you know I've been sitting here wondering who you remind me of,' said Peter Mortimer. 'I don't suppose you know me, Meredith. I remember you though, coming to the vicarage with your aunt, in pigtails.'

'I thought I'd seen you somewhere before. It's been a while since I was at Midchester. I've been living with my other aunt in Sheffield.'

'Ah, yes, I remember your aunty Sheila coming to take you away. I take it you know about Peg's broken ankle.'

For the next half an hour, Meredith talked happily with Reverend Mortimer about her memories of Midchester and visits to her Aunty Peg's cottage. 'I can still smell her strawberry jam,' said Meredith. 'And her boiled fruit cake. Aunty Sheila tries her best, but Aunty Peg got the best baking skills, I think.'

'How did your aunts come to raise you?' asked Clarice.

'My mother died during the war. She was the youngest. Aunt Sheila and Aunt Peg were in their late teens when she was born, and my grandmother died giving birth to mum. So in effect they were her mothers. Then they became mine.' Meredith smiled sadly.

'What about your father?'

Meredith shrugged. 'I don't know much about him. He died before I was born.'

Edith coughed slightly, and seemed to be about to say something, but then changed her mind. She sat with her lips tight together, in a disapproving way, contemplating her coat buttons. It occurred to Meredith that Edith knew the truth about her illegitimacy, as did the Reverend Mortimer no doubt. Not that it had ever bothered Meredith. She had been given nothing but love. Even Aunty Sheila, who was the more prim and proper of the sisters, had never treated Meredith as if she had brought shame to the family. Despite that, she found herself looking at Drew, wondering what he would think if he knew the truth.

She had also lied to her new employers. Well, not exactly lied. Just didn't tell them. She guessed that the headmistress of Willowmead Academy would not appreciate someone born the wrong side of the blanket teaching the daughters of royals and industrialists.

'Of course,' said the old policeman, sounding peeved at having lost his audience, 'vicars are the ones you've really got to watch. Have their hands in the collection box more often than not. And would kill to . . . ' He stopped talking and looked around the carriage. Drew appeared to have frozen in time, and Edith's head shot up, forgetting about her coat buttons. Even the younger people in the carriage had stopped whispering to each other and looked at the old policeman.

'Yes?' said Meredith.

'What? Oh nothing. I'm going to get a cuppa from the buffet car. Excuse me.'

2

When the old man had gone, Drew sat down in his place opposite Meredith and smiled. 'I wonder how many airings those stories have had over the years.'

'He's probably lonely,' said Meredith. 'Getting mixed up in murder, even at an official level, must help break the ice and start a conversation.'

'Humph,' said Edith. 'It wasn't much of a conversation. And accusing men of the cloth of dishonesty. I don't care what the Church of England says, or who they send . . . ' She cast a hateful look in Drew's direction. 'They won't find any wrongdoing in Reverend Mortimer's church.'

'I don't think he was accusing Peter,' said Clarice gently. 'He was merely talking in general.'

'In general indeed,' said Edith. 'He meant to cause offence, and he did. All the talk about deceitful housemaids too. It's only in fiction you get that sort of thing.' Edith stood up and left the carriage.

'Oh dear,' said Peter. 'I'd better go and calm her down.'

'Why?' asked Clarice.

'Because if she gets in a mood we shan't eat tonight.'

'I could whip us up something.' Clarice laughed.

Peter kissed her nose. 'Of course you could, darling.' He left the carriage anyway.

'I suppose I ought to go and pour oil on troubled waters too,' Clarice said to Drew. 'She's determined not to like me.' It was something that Clarice appeared to find mystifying.

'I'm going for a smoke,' said Jimmy. Betty left with him, with Bert following soon after.

'Was it something we said, do you think?' said Drew, on finding he and Meredith were alone in the carriage. 'Not that I'm complaining.'

'Are you really investigating Reverend Mortimer's church?' asked Meredith.

'Oh, you picked up on that, did you? Yes, I'm something of a troubleshooter in the Church of England. You know, travelling around, checking all is in order. Or simply taking over when some vicar has run off with an actress.' He smiled wryly. 'Not that I blame them. There have been a few discrepancies in Reverend Mortimer's church. But it'll be something quite simple, I'm sure. He doesn't seem to me to be a dishonest man.'

'No, nor to me. Not that I know him that well. I didn't even recognise him at first. It's a long time since I was in Midchester.'

'You don't know Edith then?'

Meredith shook her head. 'Not at all. Or if she was around then, I don't remember. Careful, the old man is coming back.' She heard the old policeman's voice in the corridor.

'Religious mania,' he was saying. 'People kill for religion.'

'I suppose I ought to give him his seat,' said Drew. But the man didn't come into the carriage again. He seemed content to stand in the corridor, talking to a new audience. He droned on in a monologue, hardly seeming to draw breath. Every now and then his voice rose, as he became excited by some aspect of murder. 'Wouldn't be surprised if they murdered the uncle too . . . Stole the car and went to sea, I reckon . . . Oh, about twenty thousand pounds in all . . . with a hammer then put it back on the shelf as cool as you like . . . I never forget a face . . . came to me like a flash. Luckily I'm too much of a professional to give the game away.'

Eventually his voice died down as he moved away, presumably back towards the buffet car. Meredith felt uneasy, but could not fathom why. The air seemed to crackle with malevolence.

After a few minutes, Betty and Bert appeared outside the door, and leaned against the window in the corridor.

'Have you told him yet?' asked Bert.

'No. It's like I said; I need to find the right time.' She lowered her tone. 'Jimmy's . . . well, you know what he's like. I don't want him to hurt you, Bert.'

'I can take care of myself. He flashes that knife around, but he's nothing really.'

'He's your best friend,' hissed Betty.

'You didn't think of that when . . . '

She stopped him by putting her fingers to his lips. 'Shh, do you want everyone to know?'

'Well, yeah, actually I do.'

'Don't.' Betty flounced into the carriage and sat down a couple of seats away from Meredith.

The rest of the passengers in the carriage returned, but the old policeman was nowhere to be seen. Clarice, Reverend Mortimer and Edith sat on Drew's side of the carriage, whilst the three younger passengers were on Meredith's side. Betty muttered to Jimmy, 'Where did you last have it then?'

27

'Shh, don't take on so,' Jimmy whispered. 'Bert, have you got it?'

'No, I told you. I don't know where you put it.' Bert, who was next to the door, folded his arms, and turned to look out through the carriage door into the corridor. Jimmy turned the other way, with Meredith between himself and the external window. Betty sat between them, rolling her eyes and sighing.

'I think our policeman friend has probably found a more willing audience,' said Reverend Mortimer. 'Boring some chap back there about his heyday in the force.'

'It isn't right to take that much pleasure in murder,' said Edith. 'He's as bad as Peg Bradbourne.' She clamped her lips together. 'Sorry, Miss Bradbourne, but it's the truth. Your aunty takes too much delight in other peoples' suffering.'

'My aunt is a staunch defender of justice,' said Meredith hotly. 'She believes that to take another life is the worst sin anyone can commit, and I happen to agree with her.'

'Hear hear,' said Drew, putting his hands together in a silent clapping motion.

Meredith began to wish the journey was over. There was a tension in the air which disturbed her greatly. She looked around her fellow passengers but could not tell where it originated. So instead, she gazed out of the window, and was relieved when the blue remembered hills of Shropshire began to appear.

Half an hour later they pulled into Midchester station. As she stepped out onto the platform, Meredith found herself looking back into the train, searching for the old policeman. There was no sign of him that she could see, but that didn't mean anything. He could easily be tucked away in a carriage somewhere or in one of the toilet compartments.

'I can't see him either,' said Drew. Meredith looked around at him, startled, not least because he understood what she was doing. 'Do you need any more help with that suitcase?'

'No, thank you, Reverend Cunningham . . . '

'Drew.'

'Drew. Aunty Peg's isn't far away. On Station Road in fact, in the old constable's house. Quite fitting for an elderly sleuth, yes?' Why Meredith felt the need to give him her exact whereabouts she did not know.

'Almost as if it was meant to be. Well, perhaps I'll see you around Midchester.'

'I'm sure you shall. Though I'll be with Aunty Peg a lot.' Should she invite him around? She wanted to, but shyness prevented her. She wasn't a natural when it came to chatting up men, and the fact that he was a vicar seemed to put a glass wall between them.

As Meredith spoke, the train pulled out of the station. Once again she searched for the policeman, hoping to see him in one of the carriage windows, but to no avail. All the other passengers who shared her compartment had already left the station. She could see Reverend Mortimer, his wife and their housekeeper waiting at the taxi rank. Meredith remembered that the vicarage was at the other end of the village.

'Don't worry,' said Drew. 'I'm sure he'll be tucked away in a corner somewhere, reliving his glory days with all those who got on the train at Midchester.'

'Yes, of course. And he doesn't get out till Hereford, does he? So he's got plenty of time to go through it all again. I'd better be going. Thank you again for your help.'

She was just about to pick up her case and leave the station, when the Hereford train drew to a screeching halt just beyond the station. A guard jumped off and ran back up the track, speaking to one of the porters. 'Get the ambulance and the police!' he shouted. 'There's a man injured in the toilet! He's been stabbed!'

The constable's cottage was much as Meredith remembered it, with roses around the door, and a well-stocked country garden. Not that it had been a constable's cottage for a long time. A purpose-built police station had been built at the turn of the century. But as with all small towns, the old names of buildings endured. The cottage had once been a two up two down, not counting the old jail cell at the back, which now served as a larder. It had been built onto over the years, adding a new section with an extra room downstairs, which served as the drawing room, and an extra bedroom upstairs.

'Nice place,' Drew had said, after he'd insisted on carrying her suitcase for her anyway.

'It's my favourite place in the whole world,' said Meredith, tears stinging her eyes. She was home at last. 'It's been too long since I've seen it. Thank you for helping me again. I'd invite you in, but . . . ' She didn't want him to go. She wished he would put his arm around her and tell her that everything would be all right. Which was silly. She hardly knew him. But she was shaken by what had happened to the old policeman — even though if she were honest, she had been expecting it.

'No, you go and see your aunt. You'll both have lots to talk about. I'll call on you tomorrow perhaps, to see how you are?'

'I'd like that, Drew.' Meredith let herself in through the front door, which was never locked in the daytime. 'Aunty Peg,' she called.

'Meredith! It's my darling girl! In here, in here!'

Meredith heard a chastening voice say, 'Now, now, dear, we don't want to get over-excited.'

'You might not want to, Nurse Chalmers, but I certainly do. I haven't seen her for fourteen years!'

Meredith found her aunt in the

drawing room. Aunty Peg sat on a chair near to the fireplace. 'Oh darling, come here!' She ran to kneel by her aunt, and was engulfed in lavender-scented arms. Immediately she was fourteen years younger, and ready for the type of adventure only Aunty Peg could offer.

'Oh Aunt Peg, I've missed you so much.' The tears that Meredith held back in front of Drew began to fall.

'Let me look at you.' Peg held Meredith at arm's length, and wiped a stray tear from her niece's cheek. 'You are so beautiful. Just like Mary.'

'Now,' said Nurse Chalmers, who was an efficient-looking woman in her fifties, 'I'll leave you both alone for a while, but promise me Miss Brad-bourne that you won't talk to your aunt about murders and things. We don't want her getting upset.'

Aunty Peg waited until Chalmers had gone from the room before saying to Meredith, 'Ignore her and tell me exactly why I've just heard the Hereford train stop outside the station.'

3

'He'd been stabbed in the back with the teddy boy's flick knife,' Meredith told Aunty Peg over a cup of tea and a slice of hot buttered toast. Her joy at returning to her aunt's was somewhat subdued by the awful events at the station. She had since learned that the old policeman's name was Alfred Turner. 'He'd bled to death. But Jimmy — that's the teddy boy — had gone from the station by the time they realised. I knew something would happen to Mr. Turner, as soon as he started spouting about his old cases.'

'Old policeman talk about their cases all the time, dear. Like old soldiers reliving battles. They don't all get stabbed for it.' Aunty Peg sat in a huge chintz-covered chair, with her foot, encased in plaster, resting on a stool. As far as Meredith could see, she had not changed at all. Her strawberry-blonde hair was a little greyer, but her lined face still had tremendous vitality, and her green eyes sparkled with intelligence.

'There was an atmosphere, Aunty Peg. I could feel it.' Meredith told her aunt about the old policeman's pause when he mentioned murderous vicars.

'I know of Turner,' said Aunty Peg. 'He was stationed in Hereford, but sometimes they came this far out to help us in our own enquiries, Hereford being the largest headquarters in the area. He was a rather stupid man, talked far too much about the case to all and sundry. A detective, I believe, should always keep their cards pretty close to their chest. But as I say, he's retired, and all old policemen discuss their cases.'

'He obviously never got on the same train as one of the murderers before. If that is what this is about,' said Meredith.

'You're not certain, dear?'

'The knife that killed him belonged to Jimmy. There's something going on between Betty — Jimmy's girlfriend — and his best friend, Bert. It occurred to me that if Jimmy didn't do it, then Bert might have.'

'To get Jimmy out of the way, you mean. Yes, that is possible, and more likely than Turner suddenly coming face-to-face with a killer after so many years. A bit tawdry perhaps, but murder is seldom a classy affair.'

'But,' said Meredith, who was enjoying herself far more than she felt she ought to, 'it might not be that long. He retired just ten years ago, and when he was speaking, he didn't give details of how long ago things might have happened, and he didn't mention names at all.'

'No. That makes it difficult. List for me again what cases he mentioned.'

Meredith ticked them off on her fingers as she spoke. 'There was a housemaid who murdered her employer, but too soon to get the money. Oh, before that he mentioned a man who murdered his wife but got away with it. Then some teenager who stabbed a dozen people . . . '

'We could probably halve that figure, allowing for exaggeration,' said Peg. 'Not that stabbing six people isn't bad enough.'

Meredith nodded in agreement. 'He also said something about a child. He didn't think much of children at all, and claimed that a parent was hanged for the murder of the other parent, but he thought the child did it. Then there was the bit about vicars with their hands in the till. But he was also talking to someone in the corridor. He mentioned religious mania, someone stealing a car and going to sea. Someone hitting someone else with a hammer then returning it. Oh, he said something about twenty thousand pounds before that. Then he went on about never forgetting a face, and that something had come back to him like a flash. I wasn't really listening, Aunty Peg.'

'No — that young man who carried your bag from the station was rather handsome, wasn't he? I suppose you were talking to him.'

Meredith took her aunt's teasing on the chin. 'And I thought you were in your chair the whole time,' she laughed.

'I was, dear, but it's very easy to look out of the window from here.' To illustrate, she turned slightly and proved that she had a pretty good view through the front window. 'Tell me who was in the carriage with you.'

'There was Drew.'

'Your young man.'

'He isn't my young man. He's a vicar for a start.'

'Vicars need love too. And they make very nice husbands.'

'Aunty Peg, I only met him today. His name is Andrew Cunningham, and he's a . . . what was the word he used? Troubleshooter. That's it. A trouble-shooter for the Church of England.'

'That'll be about the money in the collection box then. Old Mrs. Wheston said she put a ten-shilling note in, but when the money was counted the note was nowhere to be seen. Then there have been other discrepancies, like the church roof fund, which was five hundred pounds short.'

'Reverend Mortimer was also in the carriage, with his new wife, Clarice. He doesn't strike me as the deceitful type, Aunty Peg.'

'No, but you should be careful of discounting people because you like them, dear. I made that mistake in my early days of sleuthing. That includes the handsome Reverend Drew.' Aunty Peg's eyes twinkled.

'There was a woman called Edith too,' said Meredith, ignoring her. 'I got the impression she was Reverend Mortimer's housekeeper.'

'That'll be Edith Sanderson. She's related to us, very distantly. Her great-grandfather was labelled a lunatic. Very sad and all that, but it is sometimes hereditary, and Edith Sanderson is a strange one. Counts herself as a distressed gentlewoman. It's true some of her ancestors had money. They were architects and built many of the newer houses in Midchester. What on earth was she doing on the train?'

'She said she had shopping to do in Stockport so decided to meet them on their way home.'

'I bet she did. She's smitten with Peter Mortimer. Always has been, even during his first marriage. His wife died of pneumonia five years ago.'

'I got that impression. About Edith being smitten. She doesn't like Reverend Mortimer's new wife, does she?'

Peg grinned. 'Oh no. But everyone else does, which is what makes it so much more difficult for her. Edith, unfortunately, is not much liked at all. She's very disapproving of people. Gets all het up about the young wives who put milk bottles on the table instead of a proper milk jug. That sort of thing. People don't like to be judged nowadays.'

'Then there was Alfred Turner. The

dead man. He sat opposite me,' said Meredith, continuing with her list. 'And the three youngsters. Jimmy, Betty and Bert. Funny I'm calling them youngsters. I don't think they're that much younger than me. But they act younger. Like overgrown teenagers. They've only come up from London for the strawberry picking. If Turner was a policeman in Hereford and surrounding areas, he can't have met any of them.'

'But they may come up often, Meredith. We do tend to get the same crowd year after year.'

'I hadn't thought of that.' Meredith sighed. 'The other problem is that he didn't just speak to people in our carriage. He also had that chat with someone in the corridor, and Reverend Mortimer said he saw him talking to someone else in the buffet car.'

'No, I think you're making it too complicated, Meredith,' said Peg. 'He stopped talking about his cases to you after he mentioned deceitful vicars and had that funny turn. This suggests he saw something in that carriage. So let's confine it to there for now. I suppose we could look at past cases in the area. The problem is that the headquarters in Hereford would have covered such a wide circle.'

'And he was a policeman for a long time,' said Meredith. 'So we've no idea how long ago any of these cases happened. We could be going back fifty years.'

'Maybe more, and perhaps even further afield. You see Turner was the type to appropriate other peoples' stories as his own. I remember him talking once about having been part of a big murder trial, but when he mentioned the name, I knew it had taken place miles from Hereford. Well out of his jurisdiction.'

'But if someone tried to kill him because he recognised them, that discounts any murders that took place out of his jurisdiction,' said Meredith.

'Yes, that's a good point. But that still

doesn't mean that everything he mentioned in your carriage took place around Hereford, or really happened to him. The problem will be working out what were his cases.'

'I would think the police headquarters at Hereford could tell us,' Meredith suggested.

'Hmm, yes, but that might take too long. No, we have to do this at a local level to start with. Speak to everyone involved. People often give things away about themselves without realising. Then if that doesn't work, we'll spread the net wider. Do you know what I fancy, Meredith?'

'What?'

'A bowl of fresh, juicy strawberries.'

* * *

The following morning, Meredith, dressed in black pedal-pushers, with a pink gingham blouse tied at the waist and black plimsolls, arrived at the Bedlington Farm strawberry field. In

44

the distance she could see Bedlington Hall, which had once belonged to Colonel Trefusis, but since his death had become a boarding school for girls.

In the bright sunlight, the fields were a symphony of green and red, with sweet juicy berries ripe for picking. As well as employing travelling labourers to pick the crops for selling at the big markets, the owners also allowed locals to come in and pick their own fruit. It was under this pretext that Meredith entered the gates. She ambled through the rows of strawberries, with the air of someone who was looking for the best fruit. Really she was looking for Jimmy, Bert and Betty, though she suspected that if Jimmy knew about Turner's attack, he would not be there. Her suspicion was correct. About two hundred yards into the field, she found Betty and Bert, working alongside each other.

'Hello,' said Meredith cheerfully. 'I didn't expect to find you here.'

'That's what he said,' said Betty, gesturing to a man a little further down the row. The man wore black jeans, and a tight white T-shirt. He stood up and waved, flashing his heart-stopping smile at her.

'Hello, Meredith,' said Drew. 'I fancied a few strawberries myself.' Meredith's breath caught in her throat. The T-shirt clung to his toned body in a way that she was sure the Church would frown upon. He must be an imposter. He'd killed the real Drew Cunningham and taken his place. It was the only explanation for a man that sexy to be telling everyone he was a vicar. She would have to reveal the truth and have him arrested. It was the only way to save everyone from his devilish antics. It was the only way to save herself from the dangerously pleasurable tingling sensation in the pit of her stomach.

'We don't know where Jimmy is,' Bert said to Meredith, pulling her out of her reverie. 'He's already asked us all

46

those questions.' He jerked his thumb towards Drew.

'And we know he didn't attack the old man,' said Betty. 'So stop bothering him.'

'How can we be bothering him if we don't know where he is?' asked Meredith.

'I don't know where he is, but you should still not be bothering him.' Betty returned to her work, strawberry-picking.

'Betty,' said Meredith. She knelt down and started putting strawberries into her basket. 'Has Jimmy got any convictions? For using the knife, I mean.'

'No he hasn't. I've already told Drew that. And he should know anyway.' Betty glared at the vicar.

'Jimmy used to come to a youth club I ran in the East End of London,' said Drew. 'He's stolen a couple of cars, gone joyriding, and he fancies himself as a bit of a tough guy, but he's not a bad kid really. He just needs a bit of direction in his life.'

'Has he been coming to the strawberry-picking for long?' asked Meredith. She was speaking to Bert and Betty. 'I mean, does he know Midchester well?'

'We were all born around here,' said Bert. 'Not in Midchester. I was born in Clun, Betty in Shrewsbury and Jimmy in Crewe. But yeah, we all know Midchester.'

'So you've family in the area.'

'I never said that.' Bert looked sheepish. 'We met at the children's home in Shrewsbury, didn't we, Betty? Then when we were old enough, we decided to go and live in London. We just come back for strawberry-picking. There's not much work in London.'

Remembering what Turner said about a child whose one parent was hanged for murdering the other, Meredith asked, 'What happened to Jimmy's parents?'

'I dunno.' Bert shrugged. 'His dad ran out before he was born, and his mother couldn't cope, so she left him there.'

'What about your parents?'

'What about them?' Bert became belligerent. 'What have they got to do with anything?'

'I just wondered. What about you, Betty? What happened with your parents?'

'Meredith . . . ' Drew spoke gently. 'Could I have a quick word?'

He led her to a place several rows away from Betty and Bert. Meredith didn't like the way he folded his arms. He reminded her of the time she had done something to upset her schoolteacher. 'Meredith, I've worked with these kids for a long time. You can't just fire questions at them like that. It makes them feel guilty of something even when they're not.'

'I'm just trying to find out what happened to Alfred Turner. I'm not suggesting they're guilty.'

'They won't see it that way. All their lives they've been pushed around by authority figures, made to feel worthless because they came from a bad background. You're adding to their feelings of being victimized.'

Meredith felt her cheeks start to glow. 'I didn't mean to do that. I just wanted to ask questions.'

'If you're going to play sleuth here, you've got a lot to learn.'

'And you're an expert?'

'Maybe not at detecting, but in my line of work you learn how to get information out of people without them realising you're doing it. Whereas you . . . I'm sorry, but you're too full on. Too abrasive.'

'I am not abrasive!'

'Yes, you are. Shooting out questions like that. You should have taken the time to get to know them, and then you might find they'd tell you what you want to know.'

'Have they told you?'

'Not yet. I was waiting for the right time to open up the discussion. But I'm afraid you've probably put paid to that. They'll be on their guard now.'

'Well, Monsieur Poirot, I'm very sorry if I've queered your pitch!' Meredith stormed off down the strawberry field, and was about to leave when she remembered that her aunt really did want fresh strawberries.

She worked quietly near to the entrance. Though the best strawberries were probably further into the field, she did not want to have to face Drew again. How dare he chastise her for her methods of detecting? Obviously he thought he was in with the young crowd, because he listened to the same music as them, and let them call him Drew, but that didn't mean he had the right to tell her what to do and how to behave. She fumed silently, pulling strawberries violently from amongst the leaves.

It was only after she'd worked for about ten minutes, filling up her basket, that she admitted to herself that he was probably right. She had gone into things with all guns blazing, fired up by the thrill of the chase. She probably had a lot to learn about being a detective. Not that she was going to let Drew Cunningham put her down. She would find out who attacked Alfred Turner and prove to Drew that she was a better sleuth than him.

'I hope your aunt wanted those strawberries mashed,' Drew said. He crouched down in the lane opposite hers, looking at her over the strawberry plants. 'Whatever have they done to upset you? Or are you pretending each one is my head?' His lips curled at the corners.

Meredith looked at the strawberries in her basket. They did look somewhat bashed and beaten. Ignoring Drew, she took a deep breath and moved along the row, picking strawberries more calmly.

'Please speak to me, Meredith,' said Drew, moving along his row so that he was opposite her again. 'I didn't mean to upset you. I just wanted you to consider the way you dealt with the kids. They're terrified, for Jimmy and for themselves. They don't know if he killed Turner or not. They want to believe he didn't, because he's their friend. But even if he did stab the old man, they feel loyal to him. It's amazing what people will forgive for the sake of being loyal.'

'You seem to understand them very well,' said Meredith.

'That's because I could have been just like them.'

'In what way?' She sighed. 'Sorry, if that sounded abrasive,' she added churlishly

'Remember what I told you the other day? About us all having an Aunty Sheila? Only mine was called Gloria? You and I were lucky, Meredith. We had people to step into the role of parents when our real parents couldn't, for whatever reason. All they've had is a series of institutions with people who are kind enough, but will never feel the same love for them as a blood relation could.'

'You're an orphan too?'

'That's right.'

'What . . . ' Meredith almost asked him what happened to his parents, but was mindful of the way he had criticized her for questioning Bert and Betty.

'See,' he said, winking. 'You're learning already.' Despite his joke, he did not enlighten her as to what had happened to his parents. 'Look, there's no reason we can't investigate this together.' He said it as if holding out an olive branch.

'How do I know you're not Turner's attacker?'

'Why would I be questioning others if that were the case?'

'To find out if anyone saw you.'

'Ah, yes, I hadn't thought of that. You could be the assailant for all I know.'

'I'm not! I stayed in the carriage the whole time. Everyone else moved around.'

'Exactly, and from the time Turner left the carriage, I was in your sight. I took his seat, remember?'

Meredith had to admit that much was true. But her pride prevented her from agreeing with him. 'I'm quite capable of finding out by myself, thank you,' she said primly.

'Drew!' Bert shouted across the strawberry field. 'Come here, I want to tell you something.'

'Looks like I'll have to work alone,' said Drew.

He stood up and walked across to Bert. Meredith was sorely tempted to follow, but had the feeling Bert might clam up again if she was in the vicinity.

Sighing, Meredith picked up her basket and went to have it weighed. After she'd paid for the strawberries, she ambled back to the constable's house. She was reluctant to admit to Peg that she had failed in her first task. Then she thought about what she had learned. Not only were Bert, Jimmy and Betty born in the Shropshire area, they were all orphans, with some question over what happened to their parents. The same could be said for Drew, apart from where he was born. He hadn't offered that information. What did Aunt Peg always say? Sometimes the things people didn't tell you were as important as the things they did say.

So not exactly a bad morning's work, though she would have liked to learn more. Like what the three youngsters were up to on the train when they weren't sitting in the carriage.

'Hey, Meredith! Hold on a moment,' Drew called.

She waited until he caught up with her. 'What is it?'

'In the interests of disclosure and all that, I thought I'd share some information with you. Keep this on a fair footing. Of course I expect you to share everything you learn with me.'

'It depends how useful your information is,' said Meredith haughtily.

'Bert says he saw Turner talking to Edith Sanderson in the train corridor. And they were standing right outside the toilet compartment. They were discussing his cases, according to Bert.'

'Really? I didn't think she approved of him.'

'Obviously she only pretended to disapprove. Women like that often do feign disapproval, when it's to do with sex or violence. Secretly they love to know about it. It makes them feel superior.'

'Yes, I suppose that's true.' She remembered the gleam in Edith's eyes when she'd asked about the Mortimer's honeymoon cruise.

'She's asked me to help her out at the youth club tomorrow night. Give me an idea of how the parish does good works and all that. I don't mind if you tag along.'

'Tag along?'

'Come on, give me some credit, Meredith. I've discovered the first useful bit of information.'

'You may think that, but I couldn't possibly comment.'

'Oh, well, if you know something I don't, please do share with me.'

'Actually I don't,' Meredith admitted. 'Okay, I'll come and help out at the youth club tomorrow night.' She would never admit to anyone but herself that the real reason was that she wanted to see more of Drew.

'Great.'

'But you mustn't ask her anything until I get there.'

'Scout's honour,' said Drew, putting his fingers up to his forehead in the familiar salute of boy scouts everywhere.

'By the way,' said Meredith, before she walked on, 'since you've shared your tips with me, let me share mine with you. Aunty Peg says that you shouldn't trust people just because you like them.'

'Meaning?'

'Just because you like Jimmy, Bert and Betty doesn't mean you should take everything they say as gospel.'

'Thank you, Miss Marple. I'll remember that.'

Meredith waved over her shoulder and walked back to Peg's with a lighter step and a big smile on her face.

4

Meredith could not deny that Drew had a way with the youngsters in the youth club. They were drawn to the circle of other young people around him, as he discussed with them the music of the day, the sadness of Buddy Holly's untimely death, and the best James Dean films.

For her part, she was left standing next to a tight-lipped Edith Sanderson, who seemed to resent that the children she could not connect with had found common ground with Drew.

'Of course,' she said to Meredith as they filled paper cups with orange squash, 'it's because he's new here. Reverend Mortimer is loved just as well by his young parishioners, but he understands that children need a patriarchal society to guide them, not a brotherhood.'

Meredith was tempted to point out that Jesus preached brotherhood, but she wisely kept her own counsel. 'You've been with Reverend Mortimer a long time,' she said. 'You must have seen lots of changes.'

On their way to the village hall, Drew had coached Meredith on the importance of asking open questions. 'Never ask a question to which the answer could be yes or no,' he had said. 'That's what they call a closed question, and it doesn't always get you very far, especially with someone who's known for their reticence.'

'Not really,' said Edith. 'In Midchester changes happen slowly, and that's how we like it.'

'I admit it hasn't changed much since I was last here,' said Meredith. 'Whereas in Sheffield where I live, all the old houses have been knocked down and replaced by council estates.'

'Heaven forbid that should happen in Midchester,' said Edith. 'Though there are plans with the council for an estate

60

of that type to be built near to the railway station. With any luck we'll get them refused.'

'But people need somewhere to live, especially those who were bombed out by the war,' said Meredith.

'Let them live elsewhere. Midchester does very well as it is. It doesn't need new ideas, no matter what the vicar's new wife says.'

'I take it Clarice Mortimer is all for the new estate.'

'Well, not exactly that, but she's determined to build onto the vicarage. I mean, it's not as if she and the vicar will have children. She's far too old.' There was a gleeful tone in Edith's voice. 'The vicarage is very nice as it is.'

Meredith wanted to ask Edith about her parents, but found it much harder to come up with an open question than she realised. So she just came out with it. 'Were your parents born here?'

'No.' At least Edith's short answer proved Drew's point.

'Oh, sorry,' said Meredith. 'Aunt Peg

said you were related to us somehow, way back in time, and that our ancestors were from Midchester.'

'My great-grandfather was an architect,' said Edith proudly. 'He had family connections up here, but he wasn't from Midchester. He built many of the newer houses here. He also helped extend your aunt's cottage when it was the old constable's house. But I'm not from Midchester. The Sandersons weren't based here. They were based in Devon. That's where my mother was born, God rest her soul.'

'How long ago did she die?'

'Eighteen years ago, a few years before I came to Midchester. She'd lived to a good age. She was seventy-five.'

'That is a good age,' said Meredith. 'How long had you known Alfred Turner?'

'Who?' The question seemed to Meredith to be rather loaded. She got the impression that Edith knew exactly who she meant, but was playing dumb.

'The old policeman who was injured on the train.'

'I didn't know him at all.'

'That's odd. I thought I saw you talking to him in the corridor.'

'I wasn't talking to him.' Edith opened a packet of bourbon biscuits and tipped them out onto a plate. 'Children, your drinks are ready.' With those words, she illustrated why she did not connect with the teenagers in the village hall. They clearly did not like being referred to as children, and crossed the room sulkily. 'Just one biscuit each. Come along, don't all push in.'

'Anything?' Drew muttered to Meredith, whilst the children were busy getting their drinks. She walked away from the table and he followed, so they were out of earshot.

'No. She says she wasn't talking to him. Oh, and her mother died at the age of seventy-five eighteen years ago.'

'She must have been an old mother,'

said Drew. 'I thought Edith was about fifty-five now.'

'Yes, I think she is. They're from Devon. I don't know if that makes any difference.'

'Edith,' said Drew, going back to the refreshments table. 'I've been meaning to ask. What brought you to Midchester?'

The teenagers had dispersed and were playing games — snooker, table tennis and darts — or just near the stage area, listening to Buddy Holly on the record player.

'It's a funny story, really, Reverend,' said Edith. Despite her disapproval of him, she had a natural deference for a man of the cloth. Or probably for men in general. 'Well, not a funny story. A quite sad one really. I was supposed to come up here to work at Bedlington Hall, for a Colonel Trefusis. But he died just before I arrived. I decided to come up anyway, and luckily Reverend Mortimer and his first wife — she was such a dear lady — were looking for someone.'

'I remember that,' said Meredith. 'Colonel Trefusis's death, I mean. It was the last time I stayed with Aunty Peg.'

'It was all very cloak-and-dagger,' said Edith, managing to sound disgusted and delighted all at once. 'He was murdered, and they never found out who did it. He'd no immediate relatives, so all his estate went to a distant cousin. Twenty thousand pounds in all.'

Meredith's eyes opened wide. She exchanged looks with Drew, who nodded imperceptibly to let her know he also remembered what Turner had said to his companion in the train corridor. 'What about Bedlington Hall?' asked Meredith. 'Who inherited that?'

'No one as far as I know,' said Edith. 'The Colonel didn't own it. He rented it from the Bedlington estate. The owners live abroad I think. The other funny thing is that his car was stolen, and they never found it.'

'Of course,' Meredith said. 'I remember that, yet when I heard Mr. Turner say it yesterday, it didn't occur to me that he was talking about Colonel Trefusis. It's been so long since I thought about the colonel . . . '

'Why are you even interested?' asked Edith.

'Oh, you know,' said Meredith. 'Just trying to get some local colour, and fill in a few of the things I've missed by not being here.'

'And what about you?' Edith looked at Drew.

'Same thing. Local colour and all that.'

'Well it's nothing to do with the money going missing from the church funds, I'm sure. And if you ask me, Reverend Cunningham, I don't see why you're even looking into that. Peter Mortimer is the most honest and upright man I've ever met.'

'But the money has gone somewhere, Edith,' said Drew.

'Maybe it has, maybe it hasn't. But

I'm telling you that he hasn't taken it!' Edith's voice rose a few octaves, so that the teenagers all turned around to listen.

'Come on,' said Drew, speaking to them all. 'Turn the music up. We'll clear the snooker table out of the way and dance.'

'I don't think you should have the music too loud, Reverend Cunningham,' said Edith. 'Some say it's the devil's music.'

'I don't believe in the devil,' said Drew, ignoring Edith's stunned expression. 'At least not in a place called hell. There are more devils walking the earth.'

'What are you thinking about?' he asked Meredith, a short while later. They were dancing to a Buddy Holly song called 'True Love Ways'. Despite her trying to keep a suitable distance, he held her close to him. It was very disconcerting.

'Religious mania,' said Meredith truthfully.

'I'd hoped you were thinking of me,' he said.

'Maybe I was,' she replied, mischievously. 'You're not like any vicar I've ever met before.'

'Is that a good thing or a bad?'

'I haven't decided yet. You horrify Edith.'

'Good. It might make her think. You can't treat kids as if they're all products of the original sin, as she does. They need space to be themselves. There's a saying: if you love someone, let them go. If it's meant to be, they'll come back. That's how I believe God treats his children. Never mind how the Bible has been interpreted down the years. I've no time for all that hellfire and damnation rubbish.'

'My, you must be popular in the Church of England.'

'Why do you think they've put me in this job, which involves travelling all over the country? It keeps me out of their hair.' They danced in silence for a while. 'Now what are you thinking?' he asked.

'I'm thinking that I like the words to this song. The way it charts the highs and lows of a love affair.'

'Have you ever found true love, Meredith?'

She shook her head. 'No, but I'm not sure I'd even know what it was if I found it. I'm determined I'm not going to . . . ' She stopped there, reluctant to share with him her own thoughts on wanting a child born into a marriage, with two parents who loved it. She hardly dared admit it to herself most of the time, because she did not want to judge her mother harshly for the choices she had made. She knew, without Drew having to tell her, that she was lucky compared to Betty, Bert and Jimmy. She'd had the uncondi- tional love of Aunty Sheila and Aunty Peg, and their constant reminder that she was a special girl worthy of their love. But she also realised that too many people who knew about her beginnings judged her in the way that Edith Sanderson did. She had made a vow to herself many years before that no child of hers would be born into the same circumstances. So when boyfriends had tried to take the relationship to the next level, Meredith had pulled away, determined that she would make no mistakes that could, in the future, impact on a child. In essence she had switched off the part of herself that responded to men in a romantic way. It wasn't that she didn't sometimes find men attractive, as she did Drew, but she never let it go beyond that. She preferred to admire from afar.

'If you ever do think of me, Meredith,' said Drew, 'just try and remember that the dog collar is just an item of clothing. I'm a man, like any other man.'

It was that fact which frightened her most of all.

After the youth club had closed, Drew walked Meredith home, whilst they discussed Alfred Turner and what they had learned so far. It felt nice, walking alongside him. As if they'd known each other forever.

'I wonder,' said Meredith, 'how many more of his stories joined up. I thought he was talking about different cases, but what if the part about someone stealing the car, and the twenty thousand pounds are the same case?'

'I don't see what that's got to do with Turner being murdered now,' said Drew.

'It might if the murderer was on the train and thought he might recognise them. You said that Jimmy stole cars . . . '

'Yes, but as far as I know, he didn't have a rich uncle leave twenty thousand pounds to him. Anyway, how long ago is it that this Trefusis chap was murdered?'

'Just over fourteen years. Aunty Peg was trying to find out who'd killed him when Aunty Sheila took me away.'

'Jimmy is twenty-four years old. Yes, he might have started young, but I don't think he was even capable of murdering someone and driving away a car at the age of ten.'

'But Turner mentioned a child, one he claimed was evil.'

'Jimmy is not evil, Meredith. He's misguided, and a bit of an idiot sometimes. But he's not evil. Besides, who knows how old the child that Turner mentioned was? Bear in mind he was an old man. Anyone under eighteen would be a child to him.'

Meredith had to admit that Drew had a point. 'All the same, I might ask Aunty Peg more about Colonel Trefusis in light of what we've learned.'

'I think we're in danger of becoming sidetracked,' said Drew. 'But it's up to you, of course.'

'We have to explore all avenues,' said Meredith.

'Fair enough. Now, onto more cheerful subjects. Will you come out with me for a drink one night?' They had reached the gate to the constable's cottage.

'What? To talk about the case?'

'If we must, but I really meant you and me. As a man and woman.'

'A date?' Meredith's heart began to hammer. She felt she ought to feel safe with Drew, given his career choice, but her physical response to him told her differently.

'I'm sorry if that's such an unwelcome suggestion . . . '

'No, it isn't. I mean . . . yes, we could go on a date. It doesn't have to lead anywhere, does it?' Her mouth was so dry, she could barely get the words out.

He half-laughed, half-sighed, sounding irritated in the process. 'Not at all. In fact, if you have a drink with me just once, I promise never to darken your doorstep again.'

'I didn't mean . . . '

'Drew, Drew! Wait.' Betty came hobbling down the street on her high heels, interrupting them. 'Oh Drew, I don't know what to do.' She threw herself into his arms, sobbing. Meredith

didn't think that was absolutely necessary, frowning as Drew's arms encircled
the crying girl.

'What is it?'

'It's Jimmy. They've found him over
in Shrewsbury and arrested him. Please
come, Drew. He hasn't got anyone else.'

'I'll borrow Reverend Mortimer's car
and come straight away.' Drew seemed
to have forgotten Meredith was there.

'I could come and help,' she suggested.

Betty glared at her. 'No, not you. You
think he's attacked the old geezer. He
needs friends around him, not enemies.'

Meredith's face burned scarlet. 'I do
want to help,' she said.

'You'd best stay here,' said Drew. 'It's
not as if you know Jimmy very well.
You're practically a stranger to him.'

Meredith swallowed hard, feeling like
she was going to cry. Then, as was her
manner, she pulled herself together.
This wasn't about her feelings. It was
about Jimmy and the predicament he
was in. 'Yes, I understand,' she said.

74

'But tell Jimmy I'll do my best to find out who the real attacker is.' Betty need not know that a few minutes before, Meredith had been convinced it was Jimmy.

★   ★   ★

'What I'd like to know,' said Peg over a cup of hot cocoa, 'is how Bert knew it was Edith talking to Turner. I can't imagine he knows her. The youngsters who come up for the strawberry-picking aren't exactly churchgoers.' The drawing room was dim, illuminated only by the lamplight on the table next to Peg's chair.

'She denies it anyway,' said Meredith.

'That's not my point, dear. Boys like Bert can be suggestible. I'd like to know exactly what your Reverend Drew asked him, and what he replied.'

'You needn't worry, Aunty Peg. Drew is an expert detective.'

Peg smiled benignly. 'He's also a man with a lot of power over young minds.

He's probably too nice a person to realise it.'

Meredith sank down into the armchair. 'It's true they all love him. I'm not doing very well, Aunty Peg. No one likes me or trusts me enough to tell me their secrets. Edith disapproves of me because she knows I'm illegitimate and the youngsters just don't trust me in the way they trust Drew.'

'You're just a bit too enthusiastic, dear. I was the same in the beginning. We learn from our mistakes. All you need to learn is how to listen more to what people are saying. Really listen. Not just to what they do say, but what they don't say.'

'Yes, but if they clam up on me, what am I supposed to listen to? Drew is so approachable. Everyone talks to him, even Edith, and she doesn't approve of him either.' Meredith sipped her cocoa. 'I thought I was a nice person that other people liked until this week. Oh listen to me.' She put her cup down on the coffee table. 'A man has been murdered, and here I am feeling sorry for myself.' She couldn't explain how low she felt, and she was not sure all of it was to do with Turner's murder. She wanted Drew to be impressed with her, but she was also afraid of where that might lead. Common sense told her that she should be safe with a vicar, but then she remembered how it had felt being close to him, and his reminder that he was a man like any other men.

'The Mortimers seem to like you,' said Peg in a soothing voice. 'Clarice phoned to invite us to dinner on Saturday night, and was most insistent you go. I shan't be able to attend, but you can. They only feel bad about me because it was at the vicarage that I broke my ankle. So silly of me not to watch where I was going on the stairs.'

'Now that's where I do feel guilty. Reverend Mortimer is such a nice man, and she's absolutely lovely and charming. It seems wrong to be suspecting them of anything. I know, I know. I shouldn't discount people just because I like them.'

'Sadly no one is too nice to commit a crime. Anyone can be pushed over the edge. Assuming they're not over it already.'

'Now then,' said Chalmers, coming into the room and clapping her hands together. 'Are we ready for our bed?'

'Well, you might be ready for bed,' said Peg. 'But I think I'm going to have a tot of whisky first.'

5

If the next few days proved anything to Meredith, it was that detecting was very much a waiting game. She had expected to be rushing around, picking up clues, talking to people; but in reality, it was a matter of awaiting the chance to do all those things. She ambled around Midchester, picked more strawberries, made jam for the first time in her life, and generally got to know the area again.

She saw Drew a couple of times in the distance, but he didn't approach her, and she didn't go to him, even though she was desperate to know what Jimmy had said. She realised she was cutting off her nose to spite her face by not asking; but if she was honest, she was still irked by being left out of it all. If he wanted to tell her, he would, but he clearly did not want to share information. That's fine, thought Meredith. I'll do this on my own.

It wasn't until early on Saturday morning, when she was picking up some groceries at the corner store, that she saw him to speak to.

'Morning, Meredith.'

'Morning, Reverend Cunningham.' Meredith returned to perusing tins of baked beans on the shelf, whilst idly wondering if Aunty Peg had ever eaten them. She doubted it. Aunt Peg was very much a cook from scratch sort of person. She picked up a tin, deciding to introduce Peg to the comforting wonder that was baked beans on thick crusty toast. It would make a colourful and filling change from all the boiled eggs, rice pudding and other bland white food Nurse Chalmers forced down Peg.

'My, we are formal this morning.'

'Hmm?'

'When did I become Reverend Cunningham?'

'I thought you always were.'

'You know what I mean.' He sighed. 'Never mind. Are you and your aunt coming to dinner at the vicarage tonight?'

'I am. Aunty Peg still has to rest. Doctor's orders. Will you be there?'

'Of course, I've been staying there all week.'

'Oh.' Damn, thought Meredith, rather irreligiously. Once again, Drew Cunningham was one step ahead. He'd probably had loads of chances to talk to Peter and Clarice Mortimer. They probably looked on him as a son, and had told him all their secrets. 'I'll probably see you there then.' Meredith took the beans to the counter, along with her other purchases, and paid for them.

'Aren't you going to ask about Jimmy?'

'Yes, sorry. How is he?'

'Not bad for someone accused of killing an old man. Actually, he's in a bit of a state, given that his knife was used to kill someone. I don't think he realised until now just how dangerous a game he's been playing.'

'No, I can imagine,' said Meredith. 'Has he . . . ' She stopped, suddenly unsure of herself.

'He says that he was playing with the knife in the buffet car, then got up to go to the toilet. He thinks he must have left it on the table, but when he came back, it had gone. Betty and Bert had been sitting at the table, but they were gone too. He thought one of them must have taken it, but they deny it.'

'I suppose you've already ascertained that neither Peter or Clarice could have had anything to do with it?'

'Actually no. I've hardly seen them all week. Peter has been busy with parish business, and Clarice is arranging the summer fête. It's going to be in the grounds of Bedlington Hall next Saturday, so she's been there most of the week, making the arrangements. I've spoken to Peter about the accounts, of course, as well as the curate and others involved in the upkeep of the church. I believe they haven't got a clue where the money has gone.'

'I can't see that's anything to do with Turner's attack anyway,' said Meredith.

'Probably not, but it is the original reason I'm here. The murder is just a . . . sideshow to the Church of England, for want of a better word.'

'Oh well, I'd better be getting back.' Meredith finished loading her shopping into her bag, and started towards the door.

'Meredith?'

'Yes?'

'Peter has given me the loan of his car. I'm planning to see Jimmy in Shrewsbury this morning. Would you like to come with me?'

'Won't I be unwelcome?'

'Not if you're with me, you won't. I'd like you to hear what he's got to say and I think he'll speak to you if I'm there.'

* * *

Deep within Meredith resented that, but she put her pride aside. 'Yes, I'll

83

come. As long as Aunty Peg doesn't need me.'

'Great! And maybe afterwards we could find somewhere to have lunch. It doesn't have to be a date. In case you were worried I intended to draw you into a life of sin and debauchery.'

Shrewsbury town centre was bustling by mid-morning on a Saturday. The town was relatively unspoiled, still boasting timber framed Tudor buildings, along with other medieval landmarks. Their first stop was the police station, where Jimmy was being held, pending an appearance in the magistrates' court on Monday morning.

Meredith wore her favourite green v-necked sweater, with a full circle skirt in a grey herringbone pattern. She'd tied a pale green silk scarf around her neck.

It was only on that morning that she truly learned the power of the clergy. All the police officers deferred to Drew, allowing him access to Jimmy that might be denied to anyone else. They were shown to a tiny room, which had three chairs around a wooden table. Jimmy sat on one side, whilst Meredith and Drew sat on the other. A police officer stood in the corner, watching for any trouble.

'Here,' said Drew, sliding a packet of cigarettes across to Jimmy. 'I brought you these.'

'Thanks, Drew. You're a gent,' said Jimmy. He looked at Meredith suspiciously.

'She's alright, Jimmy. Meredith wants to help.'

'I saw you on the train, didn't I?' asked Jimmy. 'Sitting near the window.'

'That's right,' said Meredith.

'I said to Bert, she's a pretty piece. Like one of those actresses.'

She had never been referred to as a 'piece' before, but she took the compliment in the spirit intended. 'Thank you.'

'I suppose you think I hurt the old man.'

'Drew says not,' she replied. 'And

that's good enough for me.'

'Yeah, he's all right, Drew is. Not like those other stuffed shirts in the Church.' Jimmy lit a cigarette, offering the packet to Meredith and Drew.

'I'll smoke it later,' said Drew, putting one behind his ear. Meredith suspected he wouldn't — she had never seen him smoke a cigarette. It was just a way of letting Jimmy know he could be trusted.

She politely declined, saying, 'I'm trying to give them up.' She was rewarded with an appreciative glance from Drew, and a feeling that for once she had gauged it just right. 'Drew said you left your knife on the table in the buffet car.'

'Yeah, and when I come back it had gone. I thought Bert was pulling my leg. He does stuff like that.'

'Who else was in the buffet car with you?' asked Meredith, adding quickly, 'Forgive me if you've already answered this. Drew didn't tell me.'

'There was me, Bert, Betty. That old

vicar, and those two women he was with. The good-looking piece, and the old bag with a face like a bag of spanners.'

Meredith coughed and swallowed hard so as not to laugh at his description of Edith. She tried to look disapproving instead. 'No one else?'

'Well there were people coming in and out, but not when I went to the lav . . . toilet.'

'Were Reverend Mortimer and the two women still in the buffet car when you got back?'

'I can't remember. No, I think he'd gone. The two women were talking. In that really polite way people do when they hate each other's guts. The pretty one had just brought the old . . . woman . . . a cuppa, and the older one was saying, 'Oh you're so kind, Clara', or whatever her name was. But you could tell that she'd like to kill her.'

'Bert said he saw the old . . . Edith . . . talking to Mr. Turner. Did you see that?'

'No. But I wouldn't trust anything Bert says. He's stolen my girl!' Jimmy turned to Drew. 'Betty dropped it on me yesterday. Said she couldn't go on living a lie. She watches too many films that girl.'

'I'm sorry to hear that,' said Meredith. It was no surprise to her.

'Yeah, you think you know a bloke and can call him your blood brother from womb to tomb,' said Jimmy, giving the distinct impression that not only Betty watched too many films, 'then he goes and does that. I wouldn't be surprised if he hadn't stuck the old bloke so that I'd get arrested. Get me out of the way.'

'It seems a bit drastic,' said Meredith. 'They could have just told you.'

'Nah. Bert knows that if I wasn't in here, I'd probably . . . ' Jimmy stopped and clamped his hand over his mouth. The policeman in the corner was watching with great interest.

'You'd probably understand that sometimes love affairs don't last,' said

Meredith. 'All's fair in love and war and all that.'

'Yeah, yeah, that's exactly how I feel,' said Jimmy, clutching at the lifeline gratefully. 'I mean, there's other girls, ain't there?'

'Exactly.'

'And when I get out of here, I'm going to get a decent job, be a proper man. Then Betty will see what she's missing.'

'Good for you,' said Drew. Meredith wasn't sure if he was speaking to her or Jimmy.

'Jimmy is a nice boy when you get below the swagger, isn't he?' Meredith said to Drew as they walked back through Shrewsbury town in search of a restaurant.

'Yes. He's just directionless, like a lot of these kids. It probably sounds old fashioned but if he'd been set a few firm boundaries, he'd have done well in school. He's not stupid by any means, even though he sometimes acts like it.'

'You think a lot of them, don't you?

The youngsters, I mean.'

'Like I said, I wasn't that far off being just like them. You may not think it to look at me, but I went through a pretty wild period in my teenage years. I stole cars, put a brick through an employer's window.'

'Really?' Meredith looked askance at him. 'What changed?'

'I got myself into so much trouble, I daren't go home and face Aunty Gloria. I ended up spending the night in a Salvation Army hostel. There were others in there, much older than me, but they'd been on the road since they were teenagers. I asked myself whether that was what I really wanted out of life. So I went home to Aunty Gloria, confessed what I'd done, and she wasn't nearly as angry with me as I'd thought she'd be. Disappointed, yes, but angry no.'

'I realise now what a sheltered life, I've led,' said Meredith. 'Aunty Sheila protected me from everything. Too much cold, heat, rain, strangers, other people's dogs, other children. You name it, she made me afraid of it. In the end, I was frightened of my own shadow. Not that she did it to be cruel. She's not a cruel person at all. She just loved me very much. Perhaps a bit too much.'

'I've never heard anyone complain of being loved too much before.'

'No.' Meredith laughed. 'It's pretty pathetic, isn't it? Poor little me with a roof over my head, plenty to eat, warm clothes and a kind aunty and uncle to take care of me. It's a wonder I've lived to tell the tale.' She became more serious. 'The trouble is that it means I don't understand people in the way you or Aunty Peg do. I tend to make snap judgements.'

'Like about Jimmy when he sat down in your carriage on the train.'

'Yes. But he was somewhat to blame for that, Drew, flicking that knife open and closed and being offensive to Mr. Turner.'

'I'll grant you that, yes,' Drew conceded. 'Kids like Jimmy have been made to feel they've let people down all their lives. So sadly, animosity becomes their default mood.'

'But how are people supposed to know that, without knowing everyone's history? And if he's frightening people off, they're never going to learn the truth about what a nice boy he is deep down. They're always going to assume he's the thief, or in this case, the killer. It's a two way street, Drew. You have to treat others as you'd like to be treated yourself.' Meredith was unaware that her voice became more passionate as she spoke, so that people walking by paused to listen.

Drew stopped walking and looked at her thoughtfully. 'We should get you in the pulpit.'

'They don't allow women vicars.'

'That's true, and rather regretful. You'd be wonderful. But as you can't preach in church, I should let you come and speak to some of the kids one day.'

'They'd hate me for preaching at them. They like you because you don't.'

'I do, but in very subtle ways.'

'What ways?'

'I'll tell you over lunch. Come on, this looks like a nice place.' He took her into a little teashop, where they ordered salmon and cucumber sandwiches, followed by strawberries and cream.

'I listen to the songs they like, then see if I can connect the words to some teaching in the Bible,' Drew explained as they ate. 'Like 'True Love Ways'. As you say, it's all about the highs and lows of a love affair, but it could also be about the highs and lows of life. The best way to survive the low times is to have love in your heart.'

'I'd be quite interested in how you sell 'Rock Around The Clock' to them,' Meredith said mischievously.

'Oh, I just tell them that's good for dancing, and dancing is good for the soul,' he replied, smiling. He really did have a wonderful, warm smile. 'And it does mention heaven. Briefly.'

''See You Later Alligator'?'

'I've yet to find the deeper meaning

in that one, but when I do, you'll be the first to know. Bill Haley is okay, but Buddy Holly's your man for meaningful lyrics.'

'I'm an Elvis Presley fan.'

'I've a feeling that has nothing to do with his songs.'

Meredith giggled. 'I'll have you know he's a great singer.'

'Yes, he is.'

'But he is rather beautiful too.'

'He's not my type, but I'll take your word for it. I like Julie London myself.'

'Oh, 'Cry Me a River' is a wonderful song.'

'Is there anyone crying a river over you, Meredith?'

'No, I don't think so.'

'No ex-boyfriend who's going to swoop in and sweep you away from me?' His tone was silky.

'I don't . . . I haven't dated much. I . . . ' Meredith became so nervous that she accidentally knocked over her cup of tea. 'Sorry, I'm so clumsy.'

As he helped her to wipe up the

spills, their hands touched. 'Don't be afraid of me, Meredith,' he said, softly. 'I'd never do anything to hurt you.' Their eyes met across the table and it was at that moment Meredith knew she was hopelessly in love with Drew Cunningham and probably had been since her suitcase unloaded its contents at his feet. Her stomach knotted whenever she thought about him, and even the times when she'd been irritated by him, she'd still looked forward to seeing him. But where could it go? She couldn't see herself as a vicar's wife. She was far from being pious, and had never arranged a flower in her life.

They ate their strawberries and cream in silence, both lost in thought. A moment had passed between them, and neither of them knew how to move on from it. Meredith looked around the café at the other diners. Tables were piled high with delicious cakes, and the cafe had a homely feel about it, despite being in the centre of a bustling town.

In a film, she'd have realised she was in love with Drew whilst standing looking over a stormy sea with violins playing in the background. In reality, love was a warm, cosy feeling that lent itself to a place like this café, where life went on as normal, and the revelation of growing love was a quiet, and somewhat hesitant whisper rather than a crashing symphony.

'What are you thinking about?' asked Drew, breaking into her reverie.

'Violins.' The word was out before she could stop herself.

'I can't hear any.'

'No, that's the point.'

'Would you rather they were playing?'

She shook her head. 'I like things just as they are,' she replied, smiling dreamily and eating another strawberry.

'So do I.'

They paid the bill and left the cafe, each still lost in their own thoughts. Meredith had never been in love before. She wasn't sure what one did. Should she tell him? No, that wasn't a good idea. What if he didn't feel the same way? He was kind to her, and he seemed to like her, but that didn't mean anything. Drew was kind to everyone. It was what she loved most about him — his humanity, and ability to accept people for what they were, instead of what society thought they should be.

They went to Shrewsbury Cathedral. Its cool interior did wonders for Meredith's increasingly feverish head. They stood close together, but barely touching, as if to do so might break the spell between them. At least the holy place in which they walked prevented Meredith from just reaching up and kissing him.

'Now what are you thinking about?' he asked.

'Suggestibility,' she said, to cover up her true thoughts.

'Excuse me?'

'The way I was able to talk Jimmy around so that he didn't end up threatening to harm Bert in front of the police officer. I'm only a beginner, but you have a lot of power over people that you probably don't realise, because you're a nice person.'

'I'm not quite sure where this is going. Only that I don't much like it.'

'Aunty Peg thinks you might have inadvertently suggested to Bert that the woman he saw talking to Turner was Edith.'

'Hang on a minute, Meredith. I'm not an idiot. I just . . . ' Drew ran his fingers through his hair. 'Oh.'

'What is it?'

'It was me who said her name, not Bert. But he described her clearly enough, right down to her head scarf. No, no.' Drew shook his head. 'Your aunt is wrong. It was definitely Edith.' But he didn't look so sure. 'Perhaps we should go and talk to him again. Both of us. Then you can hear for yourself. Come on, we'll go back to Midchester now. Clear this up once and for all.'

'Can we go to the library first? I'd like to look up some old newspapers from this area. Aunty Peg said it's not worth it yet and to keep things local, but since we're here . . . '

They found the library and spent a while reading through all the old newspapers. They sat at a table in the centre, with Meredith on one side, and Drew at a forty-five-degree angle to her at the end.

'Shropshire seems to be a deadly place to live,' said Drew, browsing through his stack of old newspapers.

'I wouldn't say so,' said Meredith. 'These papers are spread over more than twenty years. I'm not an expert, but I suppose one murder every couple of years is average for any county, given that the murders don't all happen in one town.'

'That's still one murder every couple of years too many,' Drew said with feeling.

'Yes, I agree.' She went back to reading through the newspapers, but could not find anything that resembled the stories told by Mr. Turner. She was on the last in the pile when something caught her eye. 'Oh . . . Drew, listen to this.' Drew looked up from his own newspaper.

The headline at the top read *Husband Hanged for Murder of Wife*. The newspaper was from nineteen twenty-nine. 'Arthur Patterson was hanged in Hereford yesterday for the murder of his wife, Victoria Patterson, formerly *Trefusis*,' Meredith read, 'known as Queenie to her family and friends. Patterson was convicted of the murder late last year, after Queenie Patterson was found stabbed in her bed. Patterson confessed to the murder immediately, and refused counsel. 'Our married life was based on a lie,' said Patterson at the time. The Pattersons had a teenage daughter, Maud, who has since moved abroad and changed her name.'

'You think the daughter is the real killer?' said Drew.

'It fits with what Turner said. About a parent hanged for the murder of another parent.'

'But he said a child, Meredith.'

'You said it yourself — to him a teenaged girl would be a child. Besides, it doesn't say how old she is. She could be anything from thirteen to nineteen. But that's not the most important thing. Mrs. Pendleton's maiden name was Trefusis. I'd bet anything that she was related to Colonel Trefusis. And Turner said something about someone murdering their uncle for twenty thousand pounds, then stealing a car and driving away. Oh it's all fitting together, Drew.'

'Wouldn't people in Midchester have known if Colonel Trefusis had a relative who was murdered? It's not the sort of thing one can hide.'

'Aunty Peg said that people hardly knew him in Midchester. They hadn't had time to pry. He'd only lived there a few weeks when he was murdered. Remember, Edith was just about to start work for him. He'd barely set up his household. And even if people had connected him to Queenie Pendleton, he only had to deny it for the gossip to stop. I remember him, you know. Vaguely. He seemed at the time to be a lonely, unhappy man.'

'No, darling, I think you just believe that now because you believe he's related to Queenie Pendleton.'

'Edith would be just the right age,' said Meredith thoughtfully. She was trying to ignore the fact that Drew had called her 'darling', but the warm tingle in her spine wasn't going to let her forget.

'Don't you think Trefusis would have known if he was employing his own relative?'

'Perhaps he did know. Perhaps he just wanted to help her. Then Edith arrived earlier than she pretended, killed him, inherited his money . . . '

'Then with twenty thousand pounds in the bank, worked as a housekeeper for the vicar?'

'Yes, but she's in love with Peter Mortimer. Anyone can see that. She'd be his slave if he asked her to be.'

'Make up your mind, Meredith. She's either a matricidal witch, intent on attaining a fortune, or she's a hopeless romantic, willing to hang around the place where she's just murdered someone else so she can keep an eye on the love of her life.'

'We're not dealing with a rational person here, Drew. If she's a psychopathic killer . . . '

'Why psychopathic? I thought she murdered Trefusis for the money.' Drew frowned.

'But that's not why she killed her mother, if she did. Who knows why she did that?'

'Unless her mother had a fortune to leave her. But,' Drew ran his hands through his hair. 'Didn't Edith's mother die just before Edith came to work for Trefusis?'

'She could be lying. So that no one knows her mother died many years earlier than that.'

Drew looked at his watch. 'If we're

going to make dinner with the Mortimers, and talk to Bert first, we'd best be going.'

'Just give me a moment to write this down,' said Meredith, taking her notebook out of her handbag. 'And I need to drop in on Aunty Peg. You can come if you want. We can tell her what we know so far.'

6

When they returned to Midchester they found Betty working alone in the strawberry field. Drew and Meredith picked up a punnet each from the table at the entrance, paid their money, and went into the field.

'I'm beginning to feel like that Agatha Christie book,' said Betty, pouting. 'The one where all those people on the island die off one by one.'

'When did you last see Bert?' asked Meredith.

'This morning. We had a row . . . ' Betty paused. 'Miss Bradbourne . . . '

'Call me Meredith.'

'Meredith, can I talk to you alone for a bit? Sorry, Drew, but there's some things I can't discuss with you.'

Meredith felt a brief swell of pride. It was nice to know she had her uses.

'I'll go and pick some strawberries

for Aunty Peg,' said Drew, wandering off to another lane somewhere in the distance.

Meredith knelt down next to Betty, and started picking a few strawberries herself, so that she wouldn't get Betty into trouble. 'What is it, Betty?'

'I don't know what to do for the best,' said Betty, her eyes filling with tears. 'You see, I love Jimmy, but I think I'd be better with Bert. He's got an O-level in woodwork. And he's got plans. Wants to start up his own furniture shop.'

'That's a good plan.'

'So he'll make a better dad for my baby, you see.' Betty put her hand to her tummy.

'Oh, yes, I see,' Meredith said gently. 'But whose baby is it, Betty?'

'It's Jimmy's.'

'Does either of them know?'

Betty shook her head. 'No, I haven't said anything yet. I'm only a couple of months gone. So I could let Bert think it's his, couldn't I?'

'Do you think that would be a fair thing to do, Betty? Bert's a sensitive lad. If he ever found out the truth . . . '

'But I can't marry Jimmy,' said Betty, her voice rising hysterically. 'He's not stable. Anyway, he might be hanged for murder. I can't tell my baby that his daddy is a killer.'

'Jimmy won't be hanged if we've got anything to do with it. I think . . . I think what's happened has taught Jimmy a lesson. I've got a feeling he won't want to touch a knife ever again. He's still got a lot to learn, but perhaps finding out he's going to be a father will be the making of him. You have to give him that chance, Betty. If he lets you down, then be honest with Bert. I think you'll find Bert will want to help you, no matter who the baby belongs to. But don't start a life together based on a lie . . . Oh . . . '

'What is it, Meredith?'

'I've just thought of something. I wonder . . . Never mind. It's up to you what you do, Betty. You don't have to choose to have any father for your baby. All that will matter is that the baby is loved and cared for.'

'I don't want my baby born illegitimate,' said Betty with some passion. 'It's got to have a better life than I've had. Pushed from one home to another. Treated like dirt because . . . '

'But it won't be like that, because your baby will have a mother who loves it. A child can survive anything as long as it's loved. And I know you're going to give that child your very best.'

'You've got more faith in me than I've got in myself,' said Betty, wiping a tear from her eye.

'Well someone's got to believe in you for a change, Betty.'

To Meredith's surprise, Betty threw her arms around her. 'Thank you. I know the right thing to do now.'

Meredith got up, feeling her knees creaking slightly, and went back to Drew. He'd filled the punnet with strawberries, and was eating one of them.

'Haven't you had enough strawberries today?' she asked.

Drew stood up and offered her one. 'There's no such thing as too many strawberries.'

After they'd paid for their crops, they walked back to Aunty Peg's. The sun shone overhead, and Meredith realised that there was no better place on earth to be than Midchester in the summer. Or anytime for that matter. The back of her hand kept brushing Drew's fingers, and once or twice she was tempted to hold his hand, but shyness prevented her.

'Do you know, the sound travels quite well across that field?' said Drew.

'Oh,' she said, her heart dropping. 'What did I say wrong now?'

In response, he swept his hand around her waist, and pulled her towards him. His lips found hers, as her punnet of strawberries, looking like tiny red hearts, tumbled to the ground.

★　★　★

'Have you been running, darling?' Peg asked Meredith, when they sat in the drawing room ten minutes later. 'You look a little flushed.'

'I'm . . . oh it's a warm day,' said Meredith, trying hard not to look at Drew.

'Tell me what you've found out.'

Meredith and Drew told Peg what they'd learned that day, and how Meredith had linked it all together.

'So you think Edith is the colonel's relative?' Peg thought about it for a while.

'I'm sure that if she was, you'd have found out when you investigated fourteen years ago,' said Drew. Meredith wasn't sure, but she thought she sensed a question in his voice. Why hadn't Aunty Peg tried harder to find out about Trefusis?

'I'm afraid I failed over Colonel Trefusis,' said Peg. Her old eyes became misty. 'It was a bad year for me, and . . . well . . . the death of a man I'd only known a few weeks became less

110

important to me.'

'Because it was then that Meredith went away,' Drew suggested kindly.

'Yes. I missed her so much when she'd gone, I didn't do much of anything.' Peg wiped away a tear, and Meredith felt her own eyes stinging. 'It's the only time I've ever failed to track down a murderer, but now I realise that was meant to be. Because my girl had to come back and help me.' She smiled. 'Now, Reverend Drew, tell me all about yourself.'

'Am I being auditioned?' Drew's face broke into a smile.

'You certainly are, young man.'

'I've already told Meredith I was a naughty boy in my youth.'

'Oh I think all men should be. Actually, all young people should be. We expect far too much of our young. In fact we expect them to behave better than we ever did. Is it any wonder they rebel? Who are your parents?'

'I'm afraid I can't speak for my father,' said Drew. 'I never met him. My

111

mother was an actress . . . Or at least that's what she told her elder sister, Gloria. I'm afraid it may not have been true. She died when I was three years old, and I went to live with my Aunty Gloria, who is both terrifying and wonderful in equal measure.'

'As all aunts should be.'

'You're not terrible,' said Meredith.

'Oh that's because I didn't really bring you up, dear. Aunty Sheila did. Had I had the day to day care of you, I promise I'd have been every bit as strict as she was. As it is, I could afford to spoil you when you came to me for holidays because I didn't have to deal with the consequences.' Peg winked. 'Are you going to carry on travelling around troubleshooting or will you settle in a parish with a pretty young wife, Drew?'

'Aunty Peg!' Meredith protested. 'That's none of our business.'

'I fully intend to treat myself to a pretty young wife one day soon,' said Drew. 'As for a parish, unless I can choose Midchester, I'm not sure I'd want to be anywhere else.'

'Well, there's always hope for that,' said Peg.

'Have I passed your test . . . Aunty Peg?'

Meredith looked from her aunt to Drew, and felt she'd come into the conversation halfway through.

'Oh yes, you'll do very nicely,' said Peg. 'Now, Meredith, fetch some scones and strawberry jam from the kitchen. We'll have afternoon tea. Reverend Drew is staying, of course.' It was a command rather than an invitation, and one which Drew accepted graciously.

* * *

'I think that if I eat anymore strawberries today, I'll pop,' said Meredith, looking in the mirror over the fireplace.

Drew had left half an hour earlier, to give him time to change for dinner. He'd offered to walk back for Meredith, but she assured him she could manage to find the vicarage on her own. Since their kiss, she hadn't known what to say to him. It had been easy in the presence of Aunty Peg, who was able to keep a conversation going all on her own. But when she showed him to the door and they were alone, she became tongue-tied again. Her awkwardness increased when he kissed her lightly on the lips.

'It's the season, dear,' said Peg. 'Strawberries with everything. Never mind, Edith makes a nice strawberry flan. In fact we had that the night I went to dinner there.'

'When you broke your ankle?' Meredith tweaked an unruly curl. Her hair always refused to look as sleek as she would like it to. She wore a dress of pale green chiffon, with a tight bodice and full skirt. Around her neck, because she felt self-conscious about the low neckline, was the same scarf she had worn that afternoon.

'That's right, dear.'

'How did it happen again?'

'I was coming down the stairs, and it

was a bit dark, and there was a loose piece of carpet. Someone was behind me. I think they nearly fell too.'

'Who?' Meredith spun around. That was the first time Peg had mentioned someone else being on the stairs.

'I can't remember. I was a bit shaken, and . . . well my memory isn't what it used to be. By the time I was turned the right way up again, everyone was standing around me at the bottom of the staircase.'

'Aunty Peg, what did you talk about at dinner that night?' Meredith stopped trying to make herself look presentable and sat down opposite her aunt.

'Well, all sorts really. Of course the main topic of conversation was the loss of five hundred pounds from the church roof fund.'

'Is that why you went? To see if you could find out who'd stolen it?'

'Yes.' Peg smiled mischievously. 'It's not exactly a murder, but they don't come along every year. Thank goodness. The ten-shilling note from the collection box wasn't too serious. Sometimes there are people who'll take money out on the pretext of putting some in. Even in church, sadly. But five hundred pounds from the church roof fund. That was a different kettle of fish.'

'Did you have any suspicions?'

'Nothing definite. But well . . . the Reverend Mortimer had to pay for an expensive wedding.'

'You think the reverend stole it.'

'It did cross my mind. Middle-aged men sometimes go funny when they marry much younger wives, you know. They want to impress her so she doesn't go off with anyone else.'

'I don't think Clarice is much younger than him, is she? About ten years?'

'It's enough, and she looks younger, doesn't she? She's very glamorous.'

'Is she a resident of Midchester? I don't think I remember her from when I used to stay.'

'No. I gather her people are from

India. Or were, before it became independent. She was an English teacher at Bedlington Hall School. She met the vicar when he borrowed the grounds for last year's fête.'

'What were you doing upstairs at the vicarage? Snooping?'

Peg looked offended. 'I do not snoop, Meredith Bradbourne! Actually the downstairs cloakroom was out of order. That's the trouble with these septic tanks. So we all had to use the one upstairs. Only whilst I was in the bathroom, the landing light blew. So when I came back down, it was quite dark.'

'Aunty Peg, I want you to keep Chalmers with you whilst I'm out tonight.'

'Goodness, no, Meredith. I can't cope with that woman's twittering. She's not interested in anything but enemas and bed baths.'

'Please, Aunty Peg, for my sake. You see . . . I'm beginning to think that someone pushed you down the vicarage stairs.' To Meredith's amazement Peg's face broke into a wide smile.

'Well done, darling. I wondered how long it would take you to work it out.'

7

'Aunty Peg, this is not a game or a lesson,' said Meredith, kneeling down by Peg's chair and taking her hand. 'If you knew someone tried to . . . ' She found she could not say 'kill you', ' . . . injure you, then you should have told me immediately. Oh, I should have realised it sooner.'

'Now, now, don't distress yourself, darling.' Peg stroked Meredith's hair. 'I did rather hold back on the information.'

'Because you were waiting for me to notice, and I failed to. I'm sorry for Mr. Turner, and Colonel Trefusis and the others who have died, but you're more important to me, Aunty Peg. If anything happened to you . . . '

'Now don't cry. You'll spoil your make-up. Not that you need any. You're so much like your mother. It does my heart good to see what a lovely, intelligent young woman you've become.'

'Not intelligent enough,' said Meredith, darkly. 'I'm missing something big, and I don't know what it is.'

'There's always a final piece of the jigsaw, darling, and when you have it, everything falls into place. It's out there, waiting for you to find it. Now, you run along and don't worry about me. If someone wanted to kill me, they'd have done it by now. No, I was simply got out of the way for a while. But whoever did it, didn't bank on my successor. Go on. Don't keep Reverend Drew waiting.'

'I thought you said we shouldn't trust people just because we like them.'

'He's different.'

'How?'

'Oh well, darling, if you can't work it out for yourself, I'm not going to tell you.'

The truth was that Meredith knew exactly what Peg meant about Drew. He was different. She could no more imagine him sticking a knife into a man than Doris Day turning out to be a Russian spy. And she had to trust someone, otherwise she would go mad. It would be hard to accept there was any goodness in the world if she suspected everyone of being a cold-blooded killer. And she needed to believe there was goodness in Midchester, that it was a place worth protecting from the dark things in life. Otherwise what on earth were she and Aunty Peg fighting for?

As she walked to the vicarage, she could see that goodness. Children playing in the street, families out for an evening walk, men washing their cars, whilst women sat in deckchairs, enjoying the cool evening breeze. Meredith was sorry she would have to leave to go to Willowmead School in September. She could quite happily spend the rest of her life in Midchester. A little voice told her that she would be even happier if Drew were there too, but she pushed that aside. One kiss . . . or one and a half kisses to be exact . . . did not signify a lasting relationship. He had made her no promises, and even if his life had been much like hers, that did not mean he would choose her as a wife. She knew for a fact she would make a terrible vicar's wife. She hardly ever went to church, except at Christmas, and she would probably find it hard to get excited about polishing pews.

No, she thought, as she neared the vicarage. Best to put that idea out of her head straight away. Even if the image of her dressed in white, at Drew's side, whilst Peter Mortimer took them through their vows, kept returning to her.

The vicarage looked festive when she arrived. There were fairy lights in the trees near to the door, and when she was ushered into the hall by Edith, who took her coat, she could see through the opening that the table in the dining room was set as if for royalty, with silver cutlery and crystal wine glasses. A nagging voice that told Meredith there were people starving in the world was quickly silenced. Why shouldn't a vicar and his wife have nice things? For all she knew they'd been handed down from ancestors.

'Meredith, how lovely to see you again.' Clarice's warm smile dispelled any nerves Meredith might have had about eating in such opulent surroundings. 'I've been longing to have a proper talk with you, but I've been so busy this week, up at Bedlington Hall. Come on into the drawing room. What can I get you? A sherry? Darling, pour Meredith a sherry, will you?'

'Hello, Meredith. Nice to see you again,' said Peter Mortimer in his kindly way. He handed her a glass of sherry. 'You already know Drew, of course.'

'Yes. Hello, Drew.'

He stood with his back to the mantelpiece, nursing a glass of sherry, and frowning. 'Hello, Meredith,' he

123

said, but his mind was clearly else-where.

'Is anything wrong?' she asked.

'Drew's only worried because the car has been stolen,' said Peter.

'Oh, I'm sorry to hear that,' said Meredith. 'We dropped it off this afternoon, didn't we?'

Drew nodded, in agreement, but didn't speak.

'Oh yes, I'm sure you and Drew took good care of it,' said Peter, hastily. 'But when we returned it had gone. Edith didn't see anything, as she's been hard at work in the kitchen all day. It'll be some kids, I'm sure. Anyway, let's not allow it to spoil our evening. Let me introduce you to a few of our other guests, Meredith.'

She was treated to an array of names that she found hard to remember. There were two other couples, local landowners as far as Meredith could make out, and a woman in a tweed trouser suit. Her hair was very short, almost like a man's, and she smoked a thin cigar.

'Beth Pendragon,' she said, holding her hand out to Meredith. 'Headmistress up at Bedlington Hall.'

'It's nice to meet you.'

'Hear you're going to Willowmead in September.'

'That's right, to teach English,' said Meredith.

'Good school. Can afford to pay well, I'm sure. We could be better but not much money for staff. Most work for love. Course if we could attract decent staff, then we could charge more. Then pay more. You see how it is?'

'Erm . . . oh yes,' said Meredith, feeling she was on trial for something, but not quite sure what.

'Short one English teacher. You know what I'm saying.'

'Yes, I think so,' said Meredith, frowning. Miss Pendragon's staccato tones were somewhat hard to follow.

'Hard to get one by September.'

'Yes . . . '

'Let's all eat, shall we,' said Clarice,

dragging Meredith away. 'Ignore her, dear. She's always touting for staff. She wanted me to go back and teach, but now I'm an old married woman, I'm quite happy staying at home.'

Clarice had excelled herself where dinner was concerned. A starter of vichyssoise was followed by Dover sole, then a meat dish of venison, and topped off with a strawberry and crème anglaise flan. Cheese and biscuits were on offer for those who felt they had not had enough to eat.

Over the meat dish, Meredith chatted to Clarice. 'I hear that you and Reverend Mortimer met whilst you were teaching at Bedlington Hall.'

'That's right. It was when we had the fête last year. I helped him with many of the arrangements.' Clarice's words were punctuated by Edith slamming down a dish full of vegetables. 'Thank you, Edith,' said Clarice, waving her away. For some reason it made Meredith blush. She supposed that as she was not used to having servants, she did not know how one treated them. All the same, she felt a little sorry for Edith. 'It was love at first sight, wasn't it, darling?'

Peter was at the other end of the table. He raised his glass to his lovely wife and said, 'It most certainly was.'

'Are you from this area?' asked Meredith, despite already knowing that Clarice's family was from India.

'No, I was brought up in India. Before the independence, of course. They were magical days.'

Meredith was tempted to suggest that the Indian population might feel differently, but she liked Clarice, so did not argue the point. 'And your parents are still out there?'

'No, Mother and Father live in Malta now. The warmer climate is better for daddy, isn't it, Peter?'

Reverend Mortimer nodded and smiled.

'We called in to see them whilst on our honeymoon. We visited the Holy Lands, as part of a cruise.'

'That sounds wonderful.'

'Yes, it was.'

'Expensive, I shouldn't wonder,' said Miss Pendragon.

'Well, yes it was, rather. But you only have one honeymoon.'

'Reverend didn't. He's been married before,' said Miss Pendragon. Meredith suppressed a smile. There was something about Miss Pendragon she liked, despite the woman's abruptness. Or perhaps because of it. She had the feeling that the headmistress would always be honest, even if the truth hurt.

'How did you come to be headmistress at Bedlington Hall?' asked Meredith.

'My uncle lived in the place. Till he was murdered.'

'Colonel Trefusis?' Meredith almost dropped her glass.

'That's the one.'

'So you're his niece?'

'Said so, didn't I? Saw the place when I came up for his funeral. Thought it would make a good school. Didn't have the money then. Got some backers, and returned.'

Meredith wondered whether there was etiquette about asking whether someone had inherited a fortune. 'Did he leave you the house?' She knew that Trefusis had rented the property, but could find no other way of opening up the subject of inheritance.

'No. Rented it. Didn't leave me anything. Left it all to some girl.'

'Another niece?'

'That's what people thought. But I'm his only niece. Some young thing wrapped him around her finger, then got all the dosh. Pretty bad show if you ask me. Never met her. Would have given her a piece of my mind if I had.'

'What was he like? Colonel Trefusis.'

'Bit of a bad boy in his youth. Travelled the world. Girl in every port. Women love that. Can't see it myself. Married a girl over in India. Thought she could tame him. She couldn't. Loved her though. In the only way he could love. Never got over her death.

That's why he came here. To escape past.'

'Queenie . . . ' Drew's interruption almost made Meredith jump again. 'He was married to Queenie?'

She remembered the newspaper report. Queenie Patterson, formerly Trefusis. They'd assumed it was her maiden name.

'That's right. Victoria. Pretty little thing, so I'm told. She left him for his friend. Never saw that coming. Him being the wild one. Poor Queenie. Made the wrong choice. Then she got in with the God squad . . . sorry, Vicar.' Miss Pendragon bowed her head in Peter Mortimer's direction. 'One of those American evangelical groups. Pay us fifty pounds and we'll wipe away all your sins.'

'Religious mania . . . ' Meredith murmured, remembering something else Turner had said.

'Could call it that, yes. Poor Uncle. He might not have been faithful to her. Wouldn't have stabbed her in her bed.'

'What a charming subject for the dinner table,' said Clarice, throwing down her napkin. Edith had arrived with the desert, but stood at the end of the table listening intently to the conversation.

'Sorry, Clarice,' said Miss Pendragon. 'Life is sometimes nasty. Not like your warm, comfortable world. That's why I equip my girls for that.'

'Beth believes that girls can become doctors and lawyers,' said Peter Mortimer.

'Brain surgeons if they want to,' said Miss Pendragon.

'Don't you?' Meredith asked Peter. But she was looking at Drew when she said it.

'I'm afraid I'm the old-fashioned type, Meredith. I believe a woman's place is in the home.'

'And I happen to agree,' said Clarice. 'Which makes us the perfect couple. Doesn't it, darling? One day, Meredith, when you meet a man you fall in love with, you'll realise that all you want to do is make sure his dinner is on the table at seven o'clock sharp.'

'Of course, it helps if you've got an Edith on hand,' said Drew, picking at his strawberry flan.

'Well, yes, of course. When would I have time to make myself beautiful for Peter?' said Clarice, followed by one of her throaty laughs.

Meredith looked at her aghast. She liked Clarice, but this little woman act was almost sickening. 'I would hope,' she said, 'that the man I marry will be as supportive of my dreams as I am of his.'

'Like mine,' said Miss Pendragon. No one at the table was adept enough at hiding their surprise, apart from Clarice who obviously knew. The idea of the masculine Miss Pendragon being married at all was a bolt out of the blue.

'Beth's husband Ralph Somerville teaches woodwork at the school,' said Clarice.

'Use maiden name for career. My thing, you know what I mean.'

Meredith knew exactly what she meant. 'Where's your husband tonight?'

'Looking after our son. He's ten. Got the measles. Try not to be a fussy mother. Boys hate all that. Don't suppose you'd mind if I telephoned after dinner, though, Peter? Check my menfolk are all right?'

Meredith looked at Beth Pendragon and decided she liked her very much indeed.

'Miss Pendragon . . . ' Meredith approached the headmistress after dinner.

'Taking me up on that job offer?'

Meredith was not entirely certain she'd been offered a job, but she shook her head. 'I . . . I'd need to think about it. No, I was wondering. There's a boy I know. Drew knows him too. His name is Bert. He's got an O-level in woodwork and is looking for a job. I don't suppose Mr. Somerville needs an assistant?'

'I'll ask him. Bert, you say. One of the youngsters picking strawberries. Friend

133

of the boy who was arrested. Think I've seen him around.'

Meredith didn't doubt it. She expected Miss Pendragon to be aware of everything that was going on in Midchester. 'I don't know if Bert will even want the job, so it might be best not to say I've mentioned it. He might not want me to interfere in his life . . . '

'Understood, Miss Bradbourne. Kids like to make their own decisions.'

'What does your son want to be when he grows up?'

'A ballet dancer. Got all his certificates,' she said, proudly.

Meredith excused herself and went in search of the downstairs cloakroom. But on the way through the hall, she stopped and looked at the staircase, trying to see in her mind's eye the events that led to Peg falling down the stairs.

'She's a character, isn't she?' said Drew. Meredith hadn't realised he was standing at her side.

'Miss Pendragon? Yes, she is. I like her though.'

'Yes, so do I. Are you going to take her up on the job offer?'

'I don't know. I'm already committed to Willowmead.'

'Yes, it's a really prestigious school too. You'd be a fool not to want to work there, seeing all those young women off to their Swiss finishing schools, and onto lives of absolute uselessness as the wives of diplomats. Not a brain surgeon amongst them.'

'So you approve of women brain surgeons then?'

He didn't answer. 'Why are you staring at the staircase?'

Meredith looked around, then caught his arm and led him to the passageway between the hall in the kitchen, and out through the back door into the garden. Someone had placed fairy lights in those trees, giving the garden a warm and pretty glow. She told him in low tones about Peg's fall.

'And she's sure someone pushed her?'

Meredith nodded. 'She wouldn't imagine it, Drew. She's not that type. I'm so afraid for her.'

'Darling, she's going to be fine. We'll both keep a watch on her.' Drew stroked her cheek.

'Will we?'

'Yes, but I want you to promise me you'll be careful too. I've a feeling we're getting close to finding our answer.'

'Yes, me too. Did you pick up on all Miss Pendragon said about her uncle? I was thinking about Jimmy, Bert and Betty, and the advice I gave her today. Arthur Patterson said something about living a lie. I wonder . . . do you think it's possible that Queenie was pregnant when she left Trefusis? Then passed the child off as Patterson's?'

'And you think that when she got this religious mania, she told him? Confession being good for the soul and all that?'

'Exactly.'

'The thing is, darling, that it gives

Patterson a very good motive for killing her, and Turner seemed certain it wasn't him but the child. Why would the child murder her mother, darling?'

'Stop calling me 'darling'. It makes it very hard for me to concentrate.'

'Then allow me to ruin your concentration completely.' He pulled her into his arms and kissed her. Afterwards she rested her head against his shoulder.

'Now I can't think of anything sensible at all,' she whispered. She had never felt so content. For a moment at least, all her doubts about him were swept away. 'Apart from the fact that I'm sure it must say in the Bible that vicars shouldn't kiss like that.'

'Why do you think female parishioners keep coming back?' he said, chuckling under his breath. She slapped him playfully on the shoulder.

'So you kiss all your female parishioners, do you? I imagine your pretty young wife might have something to say about that.'

'Now why would I go out for hamburgers if I had steak at home?'

'So you liken the woman you love to a chunk of prime beef?'

'Albeit a very pretty chunk.'

She tried to pull away but he refused to let her go. 'We're getting away from what's important,' she said.

'Do you really think so? I'd have said kissing you was the most important thing in my whole life at the moment. So important, I intend to do it again.'

'No, I have to go and . . . powder my nose. Let me go, Drew.' Even she realised how half-hearted she sounded, and she did not put up too much of a fight when his lips found hers again.

By the time she finally escaped, her heart felt as light as a feather. He must like her, or he wouldn't be kissing her. But did he feel as strongly about her as she did about him? She had very nearly told him she loved him. Now she had relaxed enough to let him into her life, she did not want to frighten him away.

8

Meredith located the downstairs cloak-room. Outside stood a wooden coat rack, and she noticed Edith's coat and scarf hung on one of the pegs. Something poked out of the coat pocket — an envelope — but Meredith resisted the temptation to peek. She went into the cloakroom and tidied her hair and makeup. Her cheeks were flushed from Drew's kisses, and her eyes slightly misty. This, she thought, looking in the mirror, is what a woman in love looks like. Despite her misgivings about Clarice's little woman persona, she believed that if Drew asked her in the moment to give up everything for him, she would.

But surely, her little voice said, he wouldn't ask if he loved you. 'Yes, if he loves me,' she whispered to herself. Her feelings about him were new and untried. She understood for the first time why she had found it so easy to avoid other men until now. None of them had excited her in the way he did, both physically and intellectually. Men had a tendency to talk down to women, even more so if they suspected the woman was intelligent. Drew didn't do that. He might have felt she'd handled her interrogation badly earlier in the week, but he had told her so as an equal.

She thought about Peter and Clarice Mortimer. Did the reverend speak down to his wife? Meredith didn't think so, and yet . . . there was something odd about their relationship. That they were in love was without a doubt, but Meredith had sensed something else. A watchfulness on Mortimer's part. All through dinner, he had cast surreptitious glances at his wife, half-listening to his guests, and half-listening to Clarice. For Clarice's part, she seemed aware of her husband's attention, and occasionally raised her voice louder, or laughed for longer than necessary, as if holding his attention. It was easily done. She was a very beautiful woman.

To what lengths would a man go to keep a woman like that? Miss Pendragon had remarked on the expense of a cruise to the Holy Land. As far as Meredith knew, vicars weren't overly well paid. Unless either Peter or Clarice had a private income. Meredith further considered the luxury dinner they had just eaten, and the silver and crystal glass on the table. Clarice's dress, of gold silk, would not have been very cheap. Was it possible that Peter Mortimer, keen to keep his beautiful wife in luxury, had embezzled church funds? Meredith shook her head. She was getting away from the main issue, of who murdered Alfred Turner. Then again, Turner had mentioned that vicars were not averse to breaking the law, and it was at that precise moment he stopped talking. Did he have Peter Mortimer in mind when he said that?

Realising she had been gone some

time, Meredith slipped out of the cloakroom, bumping into Clarice as she did so. 'Oh, sorry,' she said, laughing. 'I've been much longer than I intended.'

'Don't worry. I only want to repair my make-up, otherwise I could easily have gone upstairs,' said Clarice. 'It's nice to get away from the party for a few minutes, isn't it?'

'I've had a wonderful time,' said Meredith, not wanting to seem ungrateful. 'Dinner was delicious.'

'Hmm, you must come again sometime, Meredith. Especially now you and Drew are . . . ' Clarice smiled knowingly. She winked, and said, 'I saw you in the garden.'

'Oh . . . ' Meredith found herself tongue-tied again.

'Don't worry, I shan't tease.' Clarice went into the cloakroom and shut the door. Meredith was just about to move away, when she noticed that the envelope in Edith's pocket was sticking out even further. She looked around, and then gently slid it upwards, without pulling it right out of the pocket.

It had been opened and was addressed to *Miss M. Patterson, C/O The Vicarage, Midchester*. Meredith shoved it back into the pocket, almost in shock. She would have liked to read the letter, but dared not. Instead, she calmed herself and went back to the other guests in the drawing room. Drew was deep in conversation with Miss Pendragon, whilst Peter Mortimer sat in a chair near to the fireplace, almost apart from everyone else. He looked completely exhausted, but his expression changed quickly when he saw Meredith.

'Are you feeling unwell, Reverend?' she asked him, sitting down in the opposite chair.

'No, no, just a little tired, Meredith, that's all.'

'Perhaps we'd all be better getting home . . . '

'No . . . ' His tone held a note of desperation. 'No, please don't leave yet.

We've arranged fireworks.' He spoke like a man who was about to be taken to the gallows, rather than someone looking forward to a pyrotechnic display. 'In fact, Clarice should be ready to start now. Let's all go outside, shall we?'

'What's wrong?' Drew muttered to Meredith when everyone was standing outside on the terrace.

'Why do you ask?'

'When you came back from the cloakroom, you looked like you'd seen a ghost.'

'The ghost of Maud Patterson,' Meredith whispered, as a firework illuminated the night sky.

'What?' Drew caught her arm and spun her around to him.

'Shh, you'll have everyone looking at us.' Luckily Edith was over the other side of the terrace, handing out drinks from a table. 'I'll tell you on the way home. I mean, that's if you'd like to walk me back.'

'I wouldn't trust you to anyone else.'

After the fireworks, Peter tried to persuade the guests to stay on longer, but eventually, come midnight, everyone was ready for their bed. Meredith insisted she had to get back to Peg.

'Give her our best, won't you?' said Clarice. 'We feel so guilty that she was hurt in this house, don't we, Peter?'

'Yes, most certainly. A dreadful thing to happen. Tell her that we hope she's joining our dinner parties again soon, Meredith.'

'I'm worried about him,' Meredith told Drew as he walked her home. They walked along, hand-in-hand. 'Did you notice how tired he seemed? And yet he didn't want us to leave.'

'I know. He's kept me up talking late most nights. Sometimes I've had to practically beg to be allowed to go to bed.'

'And yet he and Clarice seem happy enough, don't they?'

'Yes, besotted with each other, I'd say. As far as I can see, there's never a cross word between them.'

'Drew . . . You must have noticed the money spent on tonight's dinner.'

'I certainly did.'

'You don't think . . . '

'Of course that's what I'm thinking, Meredith. Remember, I'm a vicar too. I know how little we earn.'

'Unless Peter has a private income?' Meredith did not realise till that moment how much she wanted that to be true. If a good man like Peter Mortimer could not remain honest, what hope was there for the rest of humanity?

'No, no private income. We looked into all that, of course. Especially when we heard about the cruise. But forget Peter for a moment. Whether or not he's stealing from the church is my job to find out. What did you say about Maud Patterson?'

Meredith told him about the letter she'd found in Edith's coat pocket.

'So Edith is Maud after all?'

'It would seem so,' said Meredith. 'And Bert saw her talking to Turner. So it really ties up with her being the killer, doesn't it?'

'You sound almost disappointed.'

'It's just that tonight, when Clarice was playing Princess Grace of Monaco, I felt a bit sorry for Edith. Obviously the meal was her hard work, not Clarice's. It must be hard for her . . . Edith, I mean . . . loving Peter Mortimer so much and yet being little more than a servant.'

'That doesn't justify murder. Why didn't you confront Edith with the letter? That's what detectives are supposed to do.'

'Because I'm not convinced. It's almost as if there's too much evidence against Edith.'

Meredith was prevented from saying more on account that they had arrived at Peg's cottage.

'Drew!' Betty almost jumped out of the front door, startling them both. 'I've been waiting for you.' Meredith seriously wondered if Betty lay in wait for Drew every night!

'Then why not try the vicarage?' said Drew.

'Meredith's aunty said I shouldn't go there, but to wait for you. Drew, Bert has been run over. He's in the cottage hospital.'

'What?' Meredith and Drew looked at each other.

'Meredith, I'm sorry to run out again . . . '

'It's okay, Drew. Go to him. I can't leave Aunty Peg again. Go on, Betty.'

'I can't,' said Betty, weeping. 'I can't see him like that. It's all my fault. He said he was going away because he knew I really loved Jimmy.'

'Come on inside,' said Meredith, 'and I'll make you a cup of tea. Drew, will you come back and let us know how he is?'

'Of course, darling. I'll be back soon.'

Meredith led Betty into the drawing room and settled her in a chair. 'Is it okay if Betty stays with us tonight, Aunty Peg?'

'Of course she may. She can sleep in

the spare bedroom.'

'That's very kind, thank you,' said Betty, her lips quivering. 'I'm such a dreadful person . . . '

'No, you're not,' said Meredith, sitting at her side. 'Whatever happened to Bert wasn't your fault. Tell me all about it.'

'Well you know he went missing this morning. I still don't know why. I thought it was because he was mad at me for not making up my mind. Then they found him, and he'd been hit by a car. A hit and run they called it. He was lying there in the roadside for hours. People just drove past him, because he was down in a ditch and they couldn't see him. A man walking his dog found him, around eight o'clock tonight.' Betty gulped back a sob. 'The thing is, now I don't know if I love him or not. I wouldn't feel this bad if I didn't, would I?'

'I think your emotions are all over the place at the moment, what with Jimmy and . . . ' Meredith hesitated.

'It's alright, dear,' said Peg. 'Betty told me about the baby, and the good advice you gave her.'

'That's okay, then,' said Meredith. 'I didn't want to speak out of turn. As I said, Betty, your emotions will be all over the place. Just wait until you're calmer, and Bert is better, then you'll be better able to decide.'

Betty nodded. 'Yes, you're right. I just feel bad for him at the moment.'

'Betty, I need to ask you. About what Bert saw on the train. Drew said that Bert saw Edith Sanderson talking to Mr. Turner. The man who was killed.'

'We didn't know her name. He said the woman with the scarf, and Drew said her name.'

'The head scarf?'

'No, not on her head. Bert told me it was around her neck. Like yours.' Betty pointed to Meredith's neck. 'She was talking to him outside the loo.'

'Oh God,' said Meredith. She stood up.

'What is it, Meredith?' Aunty Peg asked.

'I'm afraid we've made a dreadful mistake. Aunty Peg, I have to go. Take care of Betty, will you? And when Drew comes back, tell him where I've gone.'

'Where are you going?'

'To the vicarage. I think Edith Sanderson might be in great danger.'

9

When Meredith reached the vicarage, it appeared to be in darkness. On closer inspection, she saw that there was a dim light coming from the drawing room. She paused near to the front door. What should she do? Knock the door and demand entrance? The worst of it was that she had no real evidence. Only a hunch that could be wrong.

What had Aunty Peg said? Don't believe or trust someone just because you liked them? And Meredith had been taken in like everyone else. No, not everyone else. Peter Mortimer may have been fooled to begin with, but his demeanour at dinner pointed to a man who had had the scales removed from his eyes.

She hesitated. Perhaps she would be better off calling the police. But what could she tell them? And anyway, that would take time, and she wasn't sure if she had time. Turner was already dead, and Bert had been run over. Edith was in danger, Meredith was sure of it. She imagined the scene in her mind's eye. Edith picking up the post from the mat, and seeing the letter addressed to Miss M Patterson. She'd have known no one of that name lived there, but maybe she had her own suspicions. Albeit based more on love and envy than evidence. So she'd read it and hidden it in her coat pocket. Why? Why not tell someone about it? Perhaps because it contained some proof. Then, when Meredith had come out of the cloak-room, the letter had been sticking out of the pocket even more. Because someone else had looked at it. But why not destroy it? Because Meredith opened the cloakroom door at that very moment.

Meredith crept around the side of the vicarage and onto the terrace at the back. The back garden still smelled of saltpeter from the fireworks. The back door was unlocked, so Meredith tiptoed into the passageway, and passed the deserted kitchen. She could hear someone talking in the drawing room, so she pressed her ear against the door.

'You do see it's the best thing for all of us, don't you?' said Clarice.

'Yes.' It was a man's voice. Peter Mortimer. Once again he sounded like a man about to go to the gallows.

'We couldn't have let her stay. She'd have come between us, Peter.'

'Where has she gone?'

'Away. Forever. She won't come back. Now drink your milk, darling, then we can get some sleep.'

'Stop!' cried Meredith, bursting through the door. 'Don't drink it, Peter.' He already held the glass of warm milk up to his lips.

'It's alright, Meredith,' he said. 'Please, go away. While you still can.'

Clarice laughed. 'That sounds a bit ominous. What are you doing here, Meredith?'

'I came to find Drew,' Meredith lied.

'He was supposed to come and see us, to tell us how Bert was.'

'Bert?' Peter raised an eyebrow. It seemed to take him all his strength to do so.

'He's been run over by a car. I'd hazard a guess it's your car, Peter.'

'Now why would that be?' said Clarice. She stood up and placed herself between Meredith and Peter Mortimer.

'Because you took it after Drew brought it back to the vicarage. I imagine you found out he mentioned seeing you talking to Mr. Turner on the train. Where's Edith?'

'She's gone away.'

'I don't believe you. I think she's upstairs in her room and that you've done something to her.'

'Why on earth would I do that?'

For the first time, Meredith saw the madness in Clarice's eyes. It was so obvious, she didn't know why she hadn't noticed it before. 'Because you're Maud Patterson. Isn't that right,

Peter?' Meredith appealed to the reverend. Still holding the glass, he ran one hand over his face, as if he hoped to wipe away all the pain and anguish.

'Yes. I swear I didn't know, Meredith. Not until we returned from our honeymoon last Saturday. She told me it all. How she'd killed Turner. Why she killed her mother and Colonel Trefusis. Even about pushing Peg down the stairs. I swear I didn't know about that till then.'

'And about stealing money from church funds?'

'Yes, that too.'

'But he stood by me,' said Clarice, 'because he's a good man. He loves me, don't you, Peter?'

'Yes. It's the worst thing I've ever had to do. Love you. I don't expect you to understand, Meredith. But she's sick.'

'And that justifies turning a blind eye to murder?' Meredith looked at him aghast. She had looked up to Peter Mortimer, but now she despised him for his weakness. 'You're a man of God,

Peter, and killing another is the ultimate sin. How can you even begin to ignore what she's done?'

'As I said, I don't expect you to understand.'

'So you're going to let Edith die. That's assuming she's still alive.' Meredith hoped that Edith had been drugged with a glass of milk, just as Clarice planned with Peter. If so, there might still be time to save her life. 'And presumably you're going to let her kill me so I don't tell anyone. Where is it going to end?'

'It's going to end with this glass of milk,' he said.

'That's the coward's way out!' Meredith snapped. 'For God's sake man, look at what she's brought you to.'

'She hasn't done it, Meredith. It was my choice. One I made last Saturday when she told me.'

All the time he was speaking, Clarice looked on triumphantly.

Meredith thought she heard a noise outside, but put it down to wishful thinking. There was no one around at this time of night. She knew she had to keep talking, to give Drew time to arrive. Then they might at least be able to manage Clarice together until the police could be called. 'Why, Clarice? Your mother, for a start. Why kill her?'

'She ruined my life,' said Clarice. 'I had a father who adored me. He would do anything for me. And she got an attack of guilt and told him that he wasn't my father. That old fool Trefusis was.'

'I don't believe you. Oh I believe you killed her after she told the truth. But that wasn't the reason. Patterson wasn't a rich man, was he?'

'Oh very clever, Meredith,' said Clarice, her lip curling. It made her look ugly. 'Very well, if you must. I deserve to have nice things. I'm beautiful. Everyone says so. And she hooked herself up to a bank clerk when my real father had thousands in the bank. Daddy . . . Albert Patterson . . . knew I'd done it, but he loved me enough to sacrifice his life for me.'

'But you've married a vicar. They don't earn much more.'

'I am capable of love, you know. Besides, vicars get other perks.'

Or, thought Meredith, maybe you're just getting too old to hook a richer man. 'Like the collection box, and roof funds?'

'Exactly.'

'What about Trefusis? I suppose you told him you were his daughter.'

'Nope, I just played on an old man's vanity. Oh, nothing untoward. I'm not into incest. But it's amazing what a man is willing to give away to a pretty young thing who hangs on his every word. He left me his entire fortune.'

'Twenty thousand pounds. But it's all gone, I suppose.'

'I like to live well. And I would have been good after that, except that idiot Turner recognised me. I saw him looking at me in the carriage.'

'So when Jimmy left his knife on the table in the buffet car, you picked it up.

I suppose when you went to fetch Edith a cup of tea.'

'That's correct,' said Clarice. 'It was very clever of me.'

'But Turner had no proof you killed your mother. Why bother killing him?'

'Because mud sticks. If he'd gone around spouting that rubbish to anyone who would listen, everyone would have suspected me. Then out in the corridor, I heard him talking about Trefusis's death. He wasn't specific, but I knew the details. I told Peter what I'd done that night. I'd always promised to be honest with him.'

'And you were sure enough of him to know he wouldn't go to the police.'

'He wouldn't and he won't. He loves me. Then Edith found that letter. It's from an old friend in India, who heard I'd moved here. The blasted idiot.'

'So you're just going to go on killing? Until anyone who can identify you is dead?'

'I don't want to do it, but I have no choice. People just keep spoiling things for me. We were happy, weren't we, darling?' Clarice turned to Peter. 'Until that gossiping old policeman opened his big mouth.'

'If you leave here tonight, and they find three dead bodies in the morning, do you really think that no one will ask questions?'

'You're not that clever after all, are you, Meredith? What do you think the fireworks were for? It's a real tragedy. One accidentally went off in the vicarage, setting fire to it. You ran in to see if you could help, but were caught in the flames. There's only one survivor. She has to move away to escape her feelings of guilt.'

'Don't you love Peter, Clarice?'

Clarice wavered a little. 'Of course I love him, but he's already on his way to not loving me anymore. I can see it in his eyes. I'd rather him die now, still loving me.'

'It isn't going to work, Clarice. My aunt knows I suspect you. She won't let my death go unpunished.'

'That foolish old woman, with her prattling and pretending to be senile. She didn't even realise I'd pushed her down the stairs.'

'She did. Perhaps she didn't know it was you, but she knew she'd been pushed. Drew will work it out too.' At the mention of Drew's name, Meredith's voice trembled. She prayed that he would get there soon. She was not sure how much longer she could keep Clarice talking. 'He's neither old nor foolish.'

'Ah, young love. It's a wonderful thing. He's not coming, Meredith. He came back here on his way to the hospital and I told him that we'd had a call to say that Bert had been taken to Hereford.'

Meredith wasn't sure if Clarice spoke the truth or not. Why would Drew have called back at the vicarage? 'Did he, Peter?' she asked.

'Yes,' said Peter. 'I'm afraid so. He needed money for the late train, and hadn't taken any with him.'

Trying hard not to burst into tears, Meredith held her chin up. It had been just over half an hour since she saw Drew. Hereford was an hour and a half away. He would still be on his way to the hospital and it would be at least two and a half hours before he returned. She spun around and tried to make a run for it, but Clarice caught her by the hair and dragged her back. 'No, you don't!' Clarice's strength was surprising. Despite Meredith's best efforts, she could not break free. She was dragged to the sofa and thrown onto it, jarring her elbow as she fell forward. Clarice pulled the scarf from around her neck, then tied Meredith's hands.

'You're going to drink milk, like Peter,' said Clarice. 'Then you won't feel a thing, I promise. Now stop struggling, you silly girl and . . .'

The drawing room was flooded with light, and a voice said, 'Let the young lady go.' From her awkward position, pushed face-first into the sofa, Meredith was able to turn her head only slightly

but it was enough to see several policemen standing by. They rushed forward
and grabbed Clarice by the arms. She
fought them like a tigress, but they
eventually overpowered her. Mean-
while, Meredith felt strong hands undo
her bonds.

'Meredith, darling!' It was Drew.
When she was upright, she threw her
arms around his neck, and held him
tight, feeling as though she had just
stepped off a boat after a week on a
stormy sea.

'I thought you were in Hereford,' she
said.

'That's what I hoped she would
believe,' he said. 'But I'm not as stupid
as Clarice thinks. I went to the cottage
hospital first, and Bert was there. He's
fine, by the way. As soon as I knew that,
I rushed back here. I happened to meet
these policemen outside.'

'We were here to tell the vicar we'd
found his car,' said one of the officers.
'And that it had been used to run down
the young man.'

'Edith!' cried Meredith. 'I almost forgot. She's upstairs. I think she's been drugged.'

'It's all right, miss,' said the officer. 'We heard all that. Someone is up there with her now. The lady is unconscious, but we're bringing an ambulance. Sorry we didn't rush in sooner, but . . . well, you seemed to be doing very well at getting a confession out of Mrs. Mortimer. We didn't like to interrupt.'

'You were wonderful,' said Drew.

'Peter,' said Clarice, who had become calmer again. 'Peter, you know I only confessed to save you, darling. Tell them the truth. About how you heard Turner's story and thought he was talking about me, even though I told him later he was being silly. So you stabbed him, didn't you, Peter? To protect me. Tell them. And the money from the church fund. You took it to keep me happy, didn't you, darling? Not that he had to. I told him that, officer.'

'Is any of what she says true,

Reverend?' asked the officer.

Peter Mortimer appeared to think about it for a while, and it was as if time stood still whilst everyone awaited his answer. He finally shook his head. 'No. None of it. She killed her mother. She killed Colonel Trefusis. Then last Saturday on the train, she killed Mr. Turner, and stole the money.'

'Peter! Peter, how could you? They'll hang me for your crime. Do you really want that? Peter!' Clarice's voice rose to a screech, as the police took her away.

10

Peg and Meredith took a walk around the garden. 'It is nice to be up and about again,' said Peg. 'These weeks have flown by.'

'Yes,' said Meredith, thoughtfully.

'No word from Reverend Drew today?'

'No, he telephoned last night. He's tried to keep me informed, but you can imagine the ructions Reverend Mortimer has caused in the Church of England. They're telling the newspapers that he had a total nervous breakdown. It's the only way to explain his behaviour.'

'Poor man . . . '

'Do you think so?' asked Meredith. 'I don't know, Aunty Peg. I understand that one can be so much in love with someone, you want to protect them. But she'd have gone on killing and he would have done nothing to stop her.'

'Oh but he couldn't have darling, even if he'd tried. Clarice believed that the moon and stars were put in place just for her. And she made others believe it too. She ... well ... I suppose she played God. Peter Mortimer fell so much in love with her, that he forgot his true God. The one he had been ordained to serve.'

'Yes, I suppose so. Look, there's Bert.'

Bert ambled across the road, and stood on the other side of the hedge. 'Miss Bradbourne ... Meredith ... I've come to let you know that Mr. Somerville up at Bedlington Hall has offered me a job as his assistant in the woodwork department. I can live on site too. My own little flat above the garages.'

'That is wonderful news, Bert. Well done!'

'He says he'll sponsor me to get some proper qualifications. Become a real teacher, like.'

'Excellent!' Meredith smiled, genuinely happy for Bert.

'It's amazing, isn't it? He just turned up at the hospital and offered me a job. Just like that.'

'Stranger things happen at sea,' said Peg mysteriously. Meredith saw her aunt look across the road. Betty and Jimmy were walking along hand-in-hand.

'I'd better go,' said Bert when he noticed them.

'Hey, Bert, mate,' said Jimmy. He and Betty crossed the road to their friend. 'Don't rush off. Look, we're okay, aren't we?' Jimmy held out his hand. 'Because good mates are hard to come by. Betty explained to me how it was. How you took care of her, when I couldn't. I owe you for that. Besides, none of us have got family, except each other, and our baby's going to need an uncle he can trust.'

Bert took Jimmy's hand. 'Mates for life, yeah?'

'Yes!' said Betty. She put her hand

over theirs. 'My two best lads, pals again. I couldn't be happier.'

'What are you to going to do now, Jimmy?' asked Meredith.

'We're sticking around Midchester. The vicarage needs a new gardener, and Edith Sanderson says she'll give me a trial,' said Jimmy. 'I like flowers.' Judging by his tone, he hadn't quite convinced himself of that, but he was obviously willing to try, for Betty and the baby's sake. 'Old Edith says she wants the garden shipshape for when the new vicar arrives.'

'Did she say who it was going to be?' asked Peg.

'No. She says she doesn't know. Anyway, we'd best be going. Got to find somewhere to live. Come on, Bert. We're going to look at the flat over the post office. There's a spare room, for if you want to stay over.'

The three young people tripped off down the street together, and Meredith wiped away a stray tear. 'It's good to see them friends again.'

'Oh Meredith,' Betty called back over her shoulder. 'You will be godmother, won't you?'

Meredith waved and nodded. 'Absolutely!'

*   *   *

Once again, Meredith was struggling with her suitcase at Stockport station, and cursing how many changes she had to make.

'Here, let me help you with that.'

'Drew!'

'Hello, darling. Where are you going?' He carried the suitcase up the steps for her.

'Home.'

'Oh.' His smile dropped.

'Why, where are you going?'

'To Midchester. I persuaded the powers that be to let me be the new vicar . . . but . . . well if you're going to be in Sheffield . . . '

'No, I told you. I'm on my way home. To Midchester. I only went back to Sheffield to fetch the rest of my things.'

'You've accepted the job at Bedlington Hall School?'

'Yes,' said Meredith, smiling. 'I thought I'd rather teach girls who might go on to be brain surgeons than girls who will only go on to host dinners cooked by downtrodden women like Edith, for the French Ambassador.'

'I've said it before, and I'll say it again — you're wonderful!'

They sat close together on the train, holding hands, as the hills of Shropshire came into view. 'It's hard to believe this is where it all started,' she said, gesturing to the carriage. Luckily they had it to themselves. 'Poor Mr. Turner. He might have been a bit of a bore, but he'd served his country. In the police force and during the Great War. He deserved to die in his bed, peacefully. Not in the toilet compartment of a train with a knife through his heart.'

'When we get back, we'll get in touch with Hereford, see if we can't arrange some memorial for him.'

'That's a wonderful idea, Drew. They'll be sure to listen to you.'

'Was Aunty Sheila too upset about your move to Midchester?' he asked.

'No, because she and Uncle Norman have decided to retire there. They'll be moving in a couple of months.'

'Wonderful. And I'm moving Aunty Gloria to a nursing home nearby. The whole family will be together.'

'The whole family?'

'Well you are going to marry me, aren't you?'

'Yes,' said Meredith, hardly believing her smile could get any bigger. 'As long as you promise me one thing.'

He kissed her nose. 'Anything you want, darling.'

'If I decide to go on a murderous rampage, you must tell on me.'

'I shall walk you to the gallows myself.'

'Yes . . . erm . . . thank you, darling.' She laughed.

'But the thing is, my love, that you'd never go on a murderous rampage.'

'Hmm, I wouldn't rule it out if you started kissing your parishioners the way you kiss me.'

'I promise I'll never want to kiss another woman as long as I live. I love you, Meredith. I've loved you since I first held your bra in my hand.'

A woman who had just been about to walk into the carriage, said, 'Well, really!' and stormed off.

'You really are far too wicked to be a real vicar,' said Meredith, laughing so much that tears filled her eyes. 'I still think you're an imposter.'

'Are you going to hand me in to the police?'

'No. Never.' She kissed him hard on the lips. 'Because if I'm being fooled, I'm quite happy to go on being fooled for the rest of my life.'

Eighteen months later

The church was full of family, friends and other well-wishers. The Reverend

Andrew Cunningham stepped forward, and took the baby boy from Meredith. 'The child's name?' he asked the parents.

'Buddy Elvis Bert Simpson,' said Jimmy, who stood behind Meredith, with his wife, Betty. The congregation laughed affectionately.

Drew christened Buddy, before handing him back to his proud parents.

Edith Sanderson stepped forward with her goddaughter, a baby girl, who had a shock of strawberry blonde hair. 'The child's name?' Drew asked.

Aunty Peg, Aunty Sheila and Aunty Gloria sat in the front pew, each looking on proudly. Even Uncle Norman shed a tear.

'Holly Mary Cunningham,' said Meredith. 'As if you didn't already know.'

'Just checking in case you'd changed your mind again,' said Drew. He smiled down at his daughter, and then at his wife, his eyes full to the brim with true love ways.

We do hope that you have enjoyed reading this large print book.

Did you know that all of our titles are available for purchase?

We publish a wide range of high quality large print books including:
Romances, Mysteries, Classics
General Fiction
Non Fiction and Westerns

Special interest titles available in large print are:
The Little Oxford Dictionary
Music Book, Song Book
Hymn Book, Service Book

Also available from us courtesy of Oxford University Press:
Young Readers' Dictionary
(large print edition)
Young Readers' Thesaurus
(large print edition)

For further information or a free brochure, please contact us at:
Ulverscroft Large Print Books Ltd.,
The Green, Bradgate Road, Anstey,
Leicester, LE7 7FU, England.
Tel: (00 44) **0116 236 4325**
Fax: (00 44) **0116 234 0205**

Other titles in the
Linford Romance Library:

MORE THAN A PORTRAIT

Diana Dennison

The uneasy balance between elation and black depression is characteristic of so many affairs of the heart. Jane was to know a little more than her fair share of both before the ending of her temporary employment at the Villa Alto Clinic under the despotic rule of the unpredictable Duncan Frobisher.

FORGOTTEN

Fay Cunningham

Driving home in the dark, Serena stops to help an injured man lying in a ditch. He mutters something unintelligible, but that is only the start of her problems. Someone is watching the apartment she shares with her brother, her mother is being particularly secretive, and police detective Jack Armstrong is convinced Serena is hiding something. Just when she thinks things can get no worse, her missing father turns up. This is definitely not the time to fall in love.